The Bay of

Lies

Murder

The Bay of

Lies

Murder

A St. James City, Florida Mystery

Mitch Grant

Disclaimer

This book is a work of fiction. It does, however, make reference to real places of business on the islands of Southwest Florida's Gulf Coast. I have attempted to describe them as faithfully as possible, recognizing, however, that I could never do justice to just how pleasant and delightful they are. I apologize in advance for any shortcomings in this regard, and urge you to visit these establishments to determine for yourself just how wonderful they actually are.

In all other respects this novel is a work of fiction. Names, characters, places, and incidents are either the product of the author's imagination or are used fictitiously. Any resemblance to actual persons, living or dead, or to actual events, locales, or organizations is unintentional and coincidental.

Finally, I want to express my appreciation to my friends and neighbors on the island who, despite the real risk that some aspects of their characters might be incorporated into one of my books, continue to be willing to associate with my wife- and occasionally- with me.

Appreciation

I specifically would like to thank Mr. Tim Fitzsimmons, President of the Useppa Island Club, for his invaluable assistance in sharing with me his knowledge and memories about events that took place on Useppa Island during the period when Useppa was used by the CIA for training members of the Brigada Asalto 2506. I also want to thank Ms. Linda Reddish for her help in arranging this meeting with Mr. Fitzsimmons.

I also want to thank Jim and Meg Morrissey for having taken me on so many successful grouper fishing trips on his beautiful boat. Specifically, I want to thank them for letting me, and my friend Dennis Sprague, accompany him on an unforgettable fishing expedition to the vicinity of the Dry Tortugas which served as inspiration for much of this book.

And, finally, I want to thank Dennis Sprague, his wife Carolyn, and his sister-in-law, DeeDee, for allowing me to use them as models for several characters in this book. Their tolerance, patience and acceptance are most sincerely appreciated, as is their friendship.

I

Dedication

This book is dedicated to my six grandchildren: Ainsley, Max, Carolina, Cooper, Christopher, and Hadley. I am so proud of you, and take tremendous delight in watching you grow, develop and find your own ways and places in the world. I hope that you will, one day, enjoy reading this story written by your crazy old grandfather.

For me reading has always provided a window to the world-offering unlimited access to knowledge, information, history, travel, entertainment, and life. I hope that you, too, will develop a love of reading.

I encourage you to educate yourselves, and then go forth with wonder, honesty, integrity, humility, an unquenchable thirst for knowledge, compassion, enthusiasm, and the courage and energy to act upon your convictions.

I love you all.

Grand Dude

Cover Art

Fish Houses at Dusk: An original painting by Mel Meo.

Mel Meo is an artist whose work embodies the peace of Pine Island, Florida- her home for more than fifty years. The painter learned to draw as a child sitting on top of abandoned Calusa Indian mounds that surrounded her family's island home. Her paintings today, still reflecting the influence and spirit of that setting, are eclectic and exuberant, bursting forth through a variety of media and surfaces, and always exhibiting the artist's spirituality.

Beyond her abilities as an artist, in my opinion, Mel is simply a good person who continually unselfishly donates her time and art to support a very wide variety of charities and causes on the island. Like her paintings, Mel is a true island treasure.

Contact her at:

Melmeostudio@yahoo.com

(239) 283-0236

Prologue

Playa Giron- Bahia de Cochinos- Cuba

April 19, 1961- Noon

"Damn it, Juan- keep your head down. The bastards know where we are!"

"Who cares, Lobo? They're just stupid kids. They can't shoot straight."

"You're probably right, Juan, but still- they might get lucky."

No sooner were those words out of Ernesto "Lobo" Valdez's mouth than a high-powered military round ricocheted off the trunk of the fallen palm behind which he and Juan were hiding. The spent bullet kicked up a geyser of coral sand as it noisily plowed into the palm frond covered ground a few feet beyond his outstretched boots.

Juan Diaz was the oldest son of what had been, before Fidel Castro came to power, one of Havana's premier sugar families- with an ancestry that proudly, and honorably, stretched back to the founding Spaniards. Ernesto Valdez and Juan were friends- they had gone to school together. Ernesto's family, in contrast, had been middle class- entrepreneurial by nature, with successful automobile repair shops providing the majority of its livelihood. In their catholic school, despite the differences in upbringings and status, the two boys- probably because of their common levels of intellect- had developed a strong friendship. While they were both intelligent and successful in school, Juan was the more intellectual of the pair- he enjoyed language and books, and loved the knowledge he found there. Ernesto, on the other hand, was more drawn to math, science, and athletics- and he excelled at sports- hence his nickname. On the field he moved gracefully, but his steps were always controlled, and somehow, when he ran, seemed almost predatory in nature. There was something in the way he moved that reminded you of a hungry, focused wolf. But, now, both of their families (at least what was left of them) were exiles. Juan's mother and siblings had managed to escape to Miami- but his father had been executed in the airport after he'd been discovered to have currency hidden in his jacket. Ernesto's mother and father, and a younger brother, had made it to Puerto Rico, where they joined the families of his father's brothers who had fled there earlier. But, Ernesto's older sister had stayed in Cuba. She believed in Fidel and Che'. She also enjoyed making love to them.

"Well, Lobo, if they're lucky that would make them better off than us. This whole invasion has turned into a shit show. First, they land us here- not, where we had originally planned to go- over by the mountains. So, now we're stuck between the stinking swamp and the bay and there's only one way out. But Fidel, of course, has that one road blocked with tanks. And, now we're almost out of ammunition from killing all those stupid kids. Our boats have been sunk, gotten stuck on the coral, or sailed off and left us. And, where the hell is our air support? We know that Fidel's only got a couple of planes, but those few are just killing us! Lobo, our own planes were supposed to take out all those before we ever landed. So, where the hell is Carlos? He was supposed to lead a flight of B-26s from Puerto Cabezas? If they'd have come we'd have been on our way to Havana by now."

"Juan, my cousin Carlos wouldn't let us down- you know that. He'd be here if he could."

"Lobo, I counted twenty B-26s on the run way when we left Puerto Cabezas. Carlos told me that he and the other pilots had been training and practicing for a year- they were armed, and ready to fly.

"Yeah, well, they damn sure better get here soon- real soon. If they don't, we're not going to make it out alive."

After that neither of them spoke for a while. They both knew the truth of what Juan had just said. The infantry companies that they'd each commanded had already dissolved by this time, ordered to attempt to escape the beach by whatever means they could. Juan and Ernie had stayed behind to give them cover as they'd crawled away. Now, as they watched the road ahead (a narrow, poorly paved, tree-lined path that was to have been their victorious route to Havana) they could see Fidelista troops working cautiously towards them. These camouflage-clad fighters moved slowly, and carefully, purposely sliding from one sheltered location to another- all the while covered by the weapons of other shielded comrades. No longer were Juan and Ernesto up against frightened military academy cadets- kids who had fought bravely as they'd played their silly war games. Neither did these stealthy soldiers look like the poorly trained militiamen that had come to fight next- just frightened peasants who'd died not understanding what they were doing. Now Juan and Lobo knew that they were up against Fidel's experienced, hardened soldiers.

Finally, Juan spoke: "Lobo, why has this gone so wrong? The Americans put this together- they recruited us, they trained us, they armed us, and they promised that they were going to support us with whatever we needed once we landed? We're talking America for God's sake- the strongest country on earth! We trusted them. So, where are those proud Yankee bastards now? It feels like they've abandoned us, just dumped us here on this damn beach- just waiting for us to be hunted down and slaughtered!"

"Juan, you're right. We *have* been abandoned. But, I don't think it was the guys that we we've been working with that let us down. I still believe they are good men. It has got to be that bastard Kennedy. My uncles in San Juan told me, despite all the grand promises that he made in his campaign to free Cuba, that he couldn't be trusted. They told me that he wouldn't have the balls to stand up to the Russians when the going got tough. And, now, it looks like they knew what they were talking about!"

"Lobo, I'll promise you one thing. If I get out of here alive, and if I find out that what you've said is true, then I will avenge the deaths of our comrades on this stupid beach. I swear an oath here and now on my dear father's grave that one day I will honor the blood of our brothers by killing John Fitzgerald Kennedy for what he's done to us! Viva Cuba!"

No sooner were those heartfelt words out of his mouth than a now well aimed round found its mark, entering Juan's temple, and then exiting the other side of this well educated head in an explosion of blood, bone, and brains.

Ernesto watched as his friend's body twitched just once before it became permanently still. Ernesto then closed his own eyes, inhaled deeply, and then shook his head, as if trying to reconcile the glorious dreams of their youths with the reality of what had just taken place. He then opened his eyes, and through hot bitter tears, stared at the limp, sand-covered, camouflage-clad, lifeless body that had previously contained the optimistic, innocent spirit of his dearest friend. In that instant, as he sadly, lovingly looked at Juan he decided how best to revenge the now wasted promise of their youths. When he spoke his voice was calm, but there could be no doubting the commitment behind those words: "Juan, my friend, you can rest easy- your oath is now my oath."

With that pledge, Ernesto Valdez began to crawl away from that stupid road- stealthily heading into the damp security of the swamp. He knew that the fight had been lost, and he understood with crystal clarity that there was no longer any reason for him to risk dying on the beach. Instead, his focus now was simply on leaving it alive so that, one day, he could honor the promise that he'd just made. Viva Cuba!

Chapter One

Gulf of Mexico- September 4, 2017

As far as I'm concerned, fishing for grouper in the Gulf is about as good as fishing gets. At least it is, if the weather's good, if you're not seasick, and if you're actually catching fish. Today, the weather was great, and the seas were smooth. (Truthfully, I simply won't go offshore if the wind is forecast to be stronger than 5 -10 knots.) But, the fish had, thus far, not been cooperating.

We'd left at 4:00 that morning- well before sunrise. We were onboard my friend Doc's 30 foot, twin engine, center console. Kenny and I were serving as crew/deckhands/ fishing buddies. Together we'd all been planning, and anticipating, this trip for weeks. While Kenny and I fished often with Doc, most of those trips were essentially nothing more than 50 mile, due west, runs out of Redfish Pass. Granted, we always caught our limit of fish- Doc had great numbers in his chart plotter- but these trips were beginning to become a little stale. We'd all agreed that we needed a little more adventure. And, that's what this trip was designed to provide.

Our plan had been to simply run southwards towards the Dry Tortugas until we used up a third of our fuel. At that point we'd fish any interesting structure that we found on the bottom (Doc didn't have any marked spots that far south), and then gradually work our way back home towards more familiar territory.

The trip down had gone well. There'd been enough moonlight so that we'd been able to easily navigate our way through San Carlos Bay, and from there into the Gulf. The only moment of excitement had come when we'd had to dodge a brightly lit shrimp boat that, coming at us on our forward port quarter, was blindly heading out to sea from Matanzas Pass. No one was in the wheel house, no one was standing watch. All we could do was shake our heads as we came to a dead stop, and watched the shrimper obliviously motor straight towards the Gulf. We could only guess he wasn't used to anyone else being out in the bay at that time of the morning.

As soon as we had gotten into the open Gulf, Doc locked our desired course into the GPS. Once we were comfortably heading south Kenny and I checked with him to ensure that all was in order, humorously cautioned him to not run into anything, and advised that he should wake us only if he really, really needed help. We then pulled from the head compartment the two bean bag chairs that we'd stored there to serve as beds during the long run south. I placed mine in the aft starboard corner, settled comfortably into it, and was soon fast asleep. Two and a half hours later I awoke as the gentle light of the morning sun announced the start of another glorious Southwest Florida day. As I came to, I heard Kenny and Doc arguing about how soon we should be able to see the abandoned LORAN tower we had targeted as the first place to drop a hook.   As they debated that issue I stole a glance at the chart plotter's screen just to confirm that we were, in fact, closing on the tower. We were. Satisfied, I checked, probably for the third time, to ensure that my gear was ready.

That had been four hours earlier. We'd yet to boat a single sizeable fish. We'd hung up on several Goliath grouper, but we'd had no success in convincing them to abandon the bottom. And, we'd been cut off by several barracuda, and a couple of small sharks. But, our fish box was still empty.

"All right, Doc," I asked, "what are we going to do now? We've tried to fish all the good looking bottom that we've found, but so far, we're not catching anything. Do you have any numbers that we can try?"

"Sorry, Jim," Doc responded. "I was really hoping that this far south, and this far out in the Gulf, we'd be able to do well. But, I agree with you. We need to give up and start heading north. I've got some numbers for some spots that are about an hour north of here."

"Have you fished them before?" Kenny asked.

"Actually, I haven't" Doc responded. "But, a Cuban guy that lives on the island gave me one of his old charts last week. It's got a bunch of fishing spots marked on it. He told me that some of them were supposed to be really good. I've been waiting for this trip to fish them."

"Was the Cuban guy a fisherman," I asked.

"Actually, no. But, before he retired, he was a boat builder. And, he said that a good friend of his, a guy that he'd built boats for over the years, had given him the chart- just before he died."

"So, why'd the Cuban guy give you the chart?" Kenny asked suspiciously. "It's been my experience that most guys don't willingly give up good numbers."

"Yeah," Doc agreed. "But, I've known the guy for a while. We've gotten to know each other well through volunteer work with the Matlacha Mariners. He's an older guy, but he still likes to help out with the sports programs for kids. Unfortunately, the last time that I saw him, he told me that he didn't have long to live either. He'd just learned that he had advanced cancer, and only, at most, a few months to live. He said he wanted to get his affairs in order, and I suppose because he knew that I liked to fish, he wanted me to have this chart."

"Do the spots look good to you?" I asked.

"Yeah! Most of them do," Doc replied.

"So which ones are we going to try first?"Kenny asked.

"There are a couple that lie along the course we need to take to get home. I'd suggest we'd try those," Doc replied.

"Sounds like a plan," I replied. "What are the spots labeled?

Doc replied, "First one says, 'Grouper Hole;' and the next one's 'Grouper Rocks.'"

"Damn, those sound promising!" Kenny exclaimed. "Let's get going. We need some fish in the box."

Chapter Two

My name is Jim Story. My wife, Jill, and I retired six years ago from careers in banking. As soon as we handed in our Bank I.D. cards we relocated to St. James City, Florida, a tiny, remote fishing village located on the southern tip of Pine Island. In many ways this little town is about all that's left of coastal Southwestern "Old Florida." There are no beaches here; no high rise condos; and no fancy, overpriced shopping and dining. A fair percentage of the fulltime population of the island still makes it living from fishing, or from guiding others to fish. A number of other locals work in the island's marinas, marine stores, or in its bait and tackle shops. Another industry of consequence is the hospitality sector, i.e., bars and restaurants. Just on our little tip of the island we have seven places to get a drink. Jill and I have learned over the years that there seem to be a lot of thirsty people here. We, of course, get thirsty, too. Our village attracts a lot of day trippers from the mainland- folks desperate for a quick fix of quaintness, and hankering for views of the water. The remaining residents are retirees- a few of whom, like us, live here full-time. The rest are 'Snow Birds.'

There are many different views among the island's full-timers about Snow Birds. Just about all understand that the winter visitors are largely responsible, one way or another, for them earning a living. For that, if for no other reason, just about everyone looks forward to their migratory return each fall. But, what no one here can understand, even after decades of experiencing it, is why these folks who come from up north, refuse, unlike those of us who live here, to drive at, or preferably slightly above, the posted fifty five mile per hour speed limit on Stringfellow Road- a nearly straight two-lane road that stretches from one end of the island to the other. This thoroughfare serves as our only major automotive transportation artery.

But, we don't have to worry about traffic jams this time of year. The months of August and September, are- even for natives- uncomfortable. It's hot here, and it's humid. Ninety five degrees on the thermometer, combined with nearly saturated levels of humidity, result in oppressive conditions. Our so-called 'Feel Like' temperatures during these months are usually well in excess of 100 degrees. Consequently, the wardrobes of those of us who live here during this time of the year never feature long pants, long-sleeved shirts, or closed-toed shoes. Heck, most of us would gladly go naked in the summer if the law, and the bugs (mosquitoes, and sand gnats), would allow it.

Mosquitoes during the summer months are not something to be taken lightly. Legends say that the early explorers and settlers of the nearby coastal islands sometimes resorted to covering themselves with sand on the beach in order to sleep at night. Even today, during the early morning and early evening hours, they can be, literally, thick. During these months most of us keep cans of insect repellant by the door to spray ourselves down before we venture outside. The black salt marsh mosquito, scientifically the 'Aedes Taeniorhynchs,' is one of the banes of our existence during the summer. These devils are fierce biters. Standing water, especially during the rainy season, greatly increases the population of these flying hellions. And, if that isn't bad enough, this is also the species that transmits the Zika virus- an awful disease recently introduced into our state, probably by the hordes of tourists that pass through Florida returning from jaunts to various parts of the Caribbean. Today, most of us still tend to joke about this disease, as we swat away 'skeeters.' But, truthfully, it is starting to become a real concern.

Another serious concern during this time of year, although certainly not a new one, is the threat of hurricanes. The geography of our state, sticking out as it does into some of the warmest ocean waters on earth, makes us likely to be impacted each year by at least one of these typhoons. More storms hit Florida each year than any other U.S. state, and since records have been kept only eighteen hurricane seasons have passed without a storm impacting the state. The history of the state has been shaped, both figuratively and literally, by these monsters. The Labor Day Hurricane of 1935 still strikes fear into the hearts of those Floridians with knowledge of the state's history. This was the most intense hurricane to make landfall in the U.S. on record. Its storm surge of 20 feet obliterated Islamorada, and destroyed nearly all the structures between Tavernier and Marathon. Over four hundred lives were lost. More recently, Category 5 "Andrew" flattened South Dade County on its way to becoming the one of the costliest hurricanes to ever hit the U.S. But, the 'Okeechobee Hurricane' of 1928 was the deadliest hurricane in North American history. It had come ashore near West Palm Beach, with winds over 145 miles per hour. While thousands of homes were destroyed there, the most severe damage resulted when the storm moved over Lake Okeechobee and pushed the lake's waters out its southern edge, flooding hundreds of square miles of farm land that bordered the Lake. The depth of the water over these fields was reported as, in some cases, 20 feet. The cities of Belle Glade, Canal Point, Pahokee, and South Bay were swept away, and at least 2,500 people drowned. Many believe that the bodies of thousands of other poor farm workers were never counted. There is still a great fear among those that live south of the Lake that the dikes now surrounding it could fail.

One denominator common to all of these storms is that they occurred in either late August, or early September. Floridians know to take storms that develop during this period seriously.

"Ya'll been keeping an eye of "Irma?" Doc asked.

"That thing is way too far away to worry about yet," Kenny advised.

"Yeah, I know. But, still, I don't like the looks of it," I countered. "The models show that thing heading in our direction."

"They sure do!" Doc offered. "And, it's getting stronger fast. I do think we need to keep our eyes on it."

"Yeah, for sure," Kenny, and I agreed. "Now, how long before we get to the Grouper Hole?"

Chapter Three

As a result of having had a very slow day of fishing, the boat's live bait wells were still full of healthy bait fish. We'd spent a couple of hours the previous afternoon catching this bait a mile offshore of Redfish Pass. We wanted to make sure we used it.

After we'd run northward for almost an hour, Doc slowed the boat, and then carefully maneuvered it towards the spot plotted in his GPS.

"All right, guys!" Doc advised. "We are now sitting over the so-called 'Grouper Hole.' Let's catch some fish."

With those instructions we began to quickly prepare our fishing rigs. Doc, and I, elected to use Pin Fish on our hooks. Kenny pursued an alternative strategy, and fastened a small Squirrel Fish onto his rig.

"Kenny," I teased, "you know it's not fair to use that "grouper candy" as bait?"

"I don't care if it's fair, or not?" Kenny replied. "All I'm worried about now is catching a big grouper. I'm getting real tired of waiting on you and Doc to put fish on board. One of us needs to step up our game. I've been dreaming about a tasty grouper sandwich for days. And, I don't intend to have to go to 'The Waterfront' to pay for one."

This good natured teasing was interrupted when Doc began to crank his reel as the rod bent downward- nearly double. We all hollered in response. There was no doubt that Doc was hooked up with a good sized grouper.

"Come on, Doc," Kenny yelled. "Don't let that thing whip you. Keep it out of the rocks."

"Whoa, man! That looks like a big one. Keep it coming," I contributed.

"This *is* a nice fish!" Doc grunted, while struggling to turn his reel.

We could tell that this was true from the way that Doc had started to gasp, and from the beads of sweat that had popped up on his brow. He continued to fight the fish for several minutes longer before he finally was able to convince it to grudgingly head towards the surface. Kenny had the landing net waiting. A moment later a beautiful 36 inch grouper was on board. More whoops, and more hollers! Kenny used his cell phone to take a picture of Doc proudly holding his catch. And, then, with that nice fish in the ice box, we returned to fishing- reenergized, and more confident than we'd been all day.

But, despite that promising start, and thirty more minutes of our most determined fishing, there were no more bites. Frustrated, Doc announced, "All right guys- pull em up. Let's go try out 'Grouper Rocks'."

Twenty six minutes later we were fishing the location suggested by the next set of coordinates. Marine charts utilize a grid system of lines- latitudes and longitudes- to fix position anywhere on the earth. Latitude is the distance north or south of the equator (an imaginary circle around the earth halfway between the north and south poles), and longitude is the distance east or west of the prime meridian (an imaginary line running from north to south through Greenwich, England). Using this grid system every location on earth can be given a numerical global address consisting of two sets of numbers- "lats" and "longs." Doc had taken the addresses of the spots marked on the Cuban's old chart, and had loaded them painstakingly into the modern electronic equivalent of traditional charts- his Garmin GPS system.

Once we arrived at our desired location we could see that the rugged bottom structure on the SONAR looked promising for fish. And, no sooner had my pin fish descended to the bottom, I was hooked up with a nice grouper. As I struggled to bring it in, Doc got another on his line. Kenny, however, had yet to have a hit. Doc and I both brought in nice grouper- both long enough to keep. Over the next half hour I brought in two 'shorts'- fish that didn't make the required length- and a nice 30 inch keeper. Truthfully, I needed the break when Doc decided to reposition the boat for another drift through this productive territory.

"Captain, it looks like the Cuban's chart is pretty good," I said. "The bottom here is crawling with fish."

"Yeah!" Doc agreed. "I'm going to have to buy Ernie a drink when I get back. I'm impressed with these spots."

"Ernie?" Kenny inquired. "That sounds like a funny name for a Cuban guy."

"I agree. But, that's what he goes by. I think his real name might be Ernesto, or something like that. It probably got anglicized over the years."

"Makes sense," Kenny agreed. "But, if I were you Doc, I think that I'd take him a bag of grouper filets to thank him. And, maybe a bottle of good rum! But, we can talk about that later. For now, let's get to fishing again. We've still got two more fish to catch before we reach our limit."

Chapter Four

Doc is a retired clinical psychologist. He and his wife, Peg, moved to St. James City from Michigan after he'd retired and sold his practice. Peg is an accomplished linguist- having taught Spanish and French. They are both great people, and both really love to fish. And, critically, they seem to like taking Kenny and me off-shore with them.

Kenny is my best friend in St. James City. He retired from a career building telephone systems around the world. His resume includes stints in Central America, the Caribbean, as well as working in various countries throughout the Middle East. And, as if those locations weren't dangerous enough, he'd also spent time installing internet platforms in Harlem, Newark, and other scenic New York City locations. He has a lot of great stories to tell.

His wife, Janice, also a retired educator, spent much of her career as a guidance counselor. I joke with Janice that she hasn't really retired since being married to Kenny is likely the greatest challenge of her career. She usually rolls her eyes at that, or ignores me. Kenny and Janice share their house with Janice's sister, Gigi. We all have lots of commiseration for what Gigi has to put up with.

These backgrounds are typical of many of the retirees on Pine Island. Folks move here to pursue their dreams of fishing, boating, or whatever other tropical fantasies they never got around to fulfilling when they were busy working. But, one of the interesting things about retirement is that folks who enter this new state of being quickly discover that they need to start to reinventing themselves- literally. After you retire, probably for the first time in your life, you've suddenly got time on your hands with nothing important to do. And, you quickly discover that just swinging in a hammock, and drinking pina coladas, quickly gets old. For most it only takes a few weeks to discover that, if they are going to remain sane (and sober), they've got to figure out some way to stay busy. In addition, and equally importantly, the identities that we all spent years carefully developing during our working careers- lives spent being bankers, doctors, teachers, or whatever, no longer mean all that much here. Truthfully, no one really cares to talk about what we all accomplished, or what we all used to be. Now, all of that stuff is just history, and it doesn't matter much anymore. We know we all lived our lives the best way we could at the time. So, in a very real sense, once you retire you do have to reinvent yourself?

Doc and I have talked some about this. He's still struggling with making the transition from his working career- a life defined by the importance of helping to make a difference in other people's lives- to his new being where accomplishment is measured only by how many fish he can catch. We haven't worked this all out, yet. In fact, all that we've agreed on is that it's a good thing that he likes to fish.

But, today was not a day for such reflections. Hurricane Irma, much to our dismay, had continued to develop. The National Hurricane Center had reported that the storm had become a Category 4- with sustained winds in excess of 135 miles per hour. And, even more troubling, the long run projections showed this monster storm was aiming straight towards Florida, and was projected to continue to strengthen. And, most troubling the NHC's Forecast Discussion indicated that there would likely not be any steering currents to nudge the storm away from this projected path. Granted, we were still five days from Irma's projected U.S. land fall, and we all knew how unreliable these forecasts can be, but for me it was now time to start taking this hurricane more seriously.

"Jill," I said, as I woke from a night of restless sleep,"I'm going to put up the hurricane shutters today. I think Irma is coming."

"That's an awful lot of work, Jim. Are you sure you want to go to all of that trouble? You know that the storms never go where the projections say that they are going to go."

"I know, but I want us to be prepared. I've seen a lot of storms in my life. And, to me, this one looks like the real thing. I don't want to wait until the last minute."

"You know, don't you, that we're going to be the first ones in town with our shutters up?

"I don't care. If that things coming our way, we're going to have a lot of stuff to do. You can blame me later if I've overreacted."

"Okay," she said, "I'll remember that. But, really Jim, when was the last time a storm- I mean a serious storm, actually came in our direction?"

"Charlie is the one that everyone on the island talks about. I think it came through in 2004. Before, that it was Donna- way back in 1960. Did I ever tell you about that? I went through that one as a kid- it was bad."

"Jim- that's my point. We haven't had a major storm hit here in a very long time. Every year we get scared about one storm, or another- but, they just never actually come here. The Weather Channel, and the Hurricane Center, do their best to get folks excited, and everyone rushes out and buys plywood, generators, tarps, and who knows what else. Then all that stuff gets returned to the store after the false alarm. I've learned not to take any of these forecasts too seriously."

"Jill, I'm glad you mentioned the generator- you know the one we bought when that tropical storm came through after we first moved here. I'm sure glad now that we didn't take it back to the store."

"Jim, when was the last time that you cranked that generator?"

"I think it was back when we thought that storm was coming. It's been sitting, of course, in the garage since then. I'm glad that you reminded me of that. I'll have to see if it'll run. And, I'll have to go get some fresh gas for it. I'll probably need another five gallon fuel jug, too. Boy, there's a lot of stuff that I've got to do to get us ready. I'm going to start making a list right now of the things I've got to do."

Jill rolled her eyes. After the many decades that we've been together she knows better than to argue with me when I get like this. Rather she just said, "Okay, Honey, you just work on your shutters. I'm going to go get my nails done. We'll look at the forecast tonight to see if they've changed it."

"Okay, Baby," I replied. "Now, I better get started. I've got a lot to do!"

Jill was right. It had been a long time since a serious storm had come our way. A lot of other folks in the State had, of course, gotten clobbered. But, Southwest Florida had seemed to be protected. In fact, things had been so quiet for us that I'd never actually put up our hurricane shutters. I knew that the heavy metal shutters for the ground floor windows, and the upper floor doors, were numbered to correspond to each opening into the house. And, that, thankfully, the windows on the second and third floors would be covered with sturdy Bahamas-shutters that would simply be folded down and secured in place with stout metal pins. But, at this point, all of this was just theory since I'd never actually gone through the process of buttoning up the house. That's one of the reasons I knew that I needed to get started early. There was no telling how steep the learning curve on this project might actually be.

But, truthfully, the day went far better than I had feared it might. Granted, it would have gone a lot faster if I'd known then that I could have used a wing nut driver in a portable electric drill to tighten the hundreds of wing nuts that bolted the metal shutters to the house. I learned about that trick the next day when I helped Kenny put up the shutters on his house. I noticed that by then most on the island had started to take the approaching storm as seriously as I was.

The fact that the storm now had winds of over 175 miles per hour, making it a strong Category 5 storm, had galvanized everyone's attention. And, ominously, the forecasted path continued to point straight at Florida.

"Kenny, what else do we need to do to get ready?" I asked.

"For one thing, we need to take the covers off of our boat lifts. There's no way that they could survive the kind of winds that they are talking about now."

"How are we going to do that, Kenny? There is no way that you, or I, can climb on the frames to loosen the bungees that hold them in place."

"Well, I've been talking to Rucker," Kenny said. Rucker was another of our friends in town. He's a semi-retired owner of a construction company. He and his wife, Lillian, had just flown down from their summer residence in Ohio to get their Florida home ready for the storm. "He says he knows some folks here on the island who do construction work. He's going to hire them to take down his covers. Said he'd have them help to take down ours, if we wanted. You want yours down?"

"You bet," I said. "One other thing, Jill's finally started to get on board with making preparations. Last night she ordered a couple of boxes of sand bags. Supposed to be here before the storm? You want some?"

"Sure. But, where could we get the sand to fill them up?"

"The Fire Department brought in a couple of dump truck loads of sand. It's piled up down at their station at the Center, free for the taking. Getting sand won't be a problem."

"Okay. That's good. Jim, what are you going to do with your boat?"

"Good question, Kenny. I'm thinking about just tying it onto the lift. What do you think?"

"A lot of people are saying we should take them off the lift, and put them on a trailer in the yard. Some people are saying, whatever you decide to do with them, fill them up with fresh water to help hold them down."

"Kenny, is that what you are going to do?"

"Probably, not. I'll think I'll just do like you said, and tie it onto the lift. But, Rucker says that he's taking his off. He's planning to trailer them up to his warehouse at the Center and store them there."

"That would be better, for sure. But, we don't have a warehouse, and I'm not convinced that the boat will be any more secure sitting on a trailer in the yard under the trees. What's Doc planning to do with his?"

"He doesn't have a trailer, so he's going to just tie it onto his lift, too."

"Remind him to tie the carriages to the pilings so that they won't swing in the wind."

"Yeah, I will. So, are ya'll going to stay here, or you planning to leave?"

"Kenny, we don't know yet. I want to run, but Jill's really concerned about leaving all her stuff. When the forecast changed yesterday towards more of an east coast event, she started to want to stay. How about ya'll? What are ya'll going to do?"

We're kind of in the same boat- still trying to decide. But, we've got access to a couple different places that we could stay at in the Cape. Some friends of ours who are up north now have said that we could stay in their houses if we wanted. There'd be plenty of room if ya'll want to join us."

"Kenny, that's mighty nice of you. I'll mention it to Jill. But, you know, given the projected path of this thing it's hard to know where to go. It could get you on the east coast; it could get you in the center of the state; or, it could get you here. I think we just keep watching it for a while."

"I understand that, Jim. But, we don't want to wait too long to decide to get out. The roads will be clogged up if we're not careful."

"No doubt. I'll tell you one thing for sure, though, Kenny. If that storm starts to look like its coming here, or to the west of us, we'll cut and run. There's an old saying about storms in Florida- 'Hide from the wind; Run from the water!' If the eye comes here, or passes to the west, a damn storm surge is going to cover this entire island. And, if that happens there won't be much left of this place."

"Come on, Jim, don't be so dang cheerful! Now, I'll let you know when Rucker gets those guys lined up to work on the lift covers. Let me know if those sand bags show up."

"Okay, Kenny. You, let me know if you need any more help. I'll talk to Jill about going with ya'll."

Chapter Five

The next day was a flurry of activity. Kenny and I helped Rucker and his crew remove everyone's boat lift covers. The key to the success of this project was the sturdy aluminum plank that Rucker provided to extend across the distant ends of the boat cover's frames. This metal board served as a secure platform for the two young, limber, fearless construction workers to clamber around under the lifts' covers to remove the securing bungee cords. All the old retired guys, except for Rucker, stayed on the ground, pulled the tarps off the frames, and folded them into manageable bundles. Rucker, having spent a life time of crawling over the framework of buildings he was putting up, was reluctant to relinquish the thrill of being off the ground to a couple of young Turks.

It took all morning to remove the five covers that we'd targeted to take off. The only really challenging part of this activity was dealing with the day's extreme heat and humidity. It was as bad as any that I'd ever experienced. After we finished each project we had to take a few minutes to stand in the shade of whatever trees were handy, gulp down ice cold bottles of water from the cooler that Lillian had thoughtfully provided, and try to mop away torrents of perspiration from our faces.

"Damn, guys," I said to no one in particular, "the next time we decide to do this we need to pick a cooler day."

At that one of the construction guys spoke up. "This is just like it was before 'Charlie' came. That day, and today, are the hottest days that I can ever remember."

"Well, heck," Kenny replied, "I guess that means that 'Irma' is definitely coming here."

"I hope not," Rucker responded.

Trying to lighten the mood, I replied, "Well, I'd hate to go to all this effort, and miss the storm."

Nobody laughed.

After that, we spent time helping one another put cinder blocks under any ground floor furniture at risk of being flooded. When I got back to the house for lunch, Jill told me that UPS had delivered a partial order of the sand bags that we'd ordered- only forty bags, not the hundred that we'd wanted. But, forty were better than nothing. As soon as we'd finished eating Jill and I put the bags and a shovel into our truck, and headed to the Fire Station. Several of our Pine Island neighbors were already there, diligently shoveling sand. I noticed some were simply filling Winn Dixie plastic grocery bags. I thought that was clever. Despite the threat that we all faced everyone seemed to be in a good mood. An hour later we'd filled our forty bags. Jill had done most of the shoveling, while I'd held the bags open, tied them shut when they were full, and then carried them to the truck. In case you don't know, a bag of sand is not light.

We then drove back down the island, stopped by Kenny and Janice's house, and unloaded twenty bags for their use. At our house I carefully arranged the remaining bags in front of our pool-front glass sliders. Another item checked off the 'to do' list, and another day closer to the projected arrival of what by now had become the strongest Atlantic hurricane in history.

By this time, everyone on the island's attention was exclusively focused on Irma. Rather, I should say 'everyone still on the island.' Many had simply buttoned up their houses, and left town- not wanting any part of the gigantic typhoon that was now bearing down on us.

I spent the next morning tying down patio and dock furniture, and putting planters, and other items at risk of blowing away, into the garage. Afterwards, Jill and I feeling that we had done all we could do to prepare for the storm spent the rest of the day helping neighbors and friends who still had things to do. Rucker was nailing plywood on the upper story windows of his stilt house. Kenny was emptying out the items under his Tiki hut. We helped an elderly lady, who lived down the street, move patio furniture into her garage. There was no shortage of ways for neighbors to help neighbors, and there was no shortage of Pine Islanders willing to help. Most people seemed to be in good spirits despite the threat bearing down on us. A form of 'gallows humor' I guessed.

By now, there was little time left to decide whether to leave the island, or not. Jill was still resistant to the idea of leaving our house- I think she had developed a case of 'I'm going to go down with the ship.' Her position had been reinforced by the Hurricane Center's forecast that still showed the storm's most likely track to come up the east side of the State. Granted, we were well within the 'cone of uncertainty,' but we'd all been there before. We were starting to feel sorry for our friends that lived on that side of the state. The day before the Governor had ordered the mass evacuation of Dade and Broward counties. The Keys' evacuation had been begun days earlier. There was still no evacuation order in place for our area, although those who lived in low lying areas were being advised to move to higher ground.

St James City is definitely a 'low lying area!' We are categorized as being in Flood Zone 1, i.e., that part of the county most likely to flood. Even with normal high tides, our roadside ditches fill with salt water. And, when we have a so-called 'Spring Tide' (when the moon, earth, and sun align) many of us have water in our yards. Storm surge here is definitely something to be taken seriously. And, we all understood that the greatest risk would occur if a storm came when the tide was already high. Six to ten feet of water on top of a high tide would clearly inundate most of the island. But, this type of flooding could only occur if the storm came at us from the south, with its counter-cyclical cyclonic wind circulation blowing water from the Gulf into San Carlos Bay. What we most feared was a storm that tracked directly over, or slightly to the west, of Pine Island; the further east the storm passed, the better off we would be.

For the last few afternoons many of those left on the island had taken to gathering at the Low Key Tiki to drink, to relax, to unwind, to check on their fellow islanders, and to discuss the approaching storm. Increasingly, the primary discussion point had become: 'Ya'll going to stay?'

Some said yes. Some said they didn't know. Some, as evidenced by each evening's shrinking crowd size, had already left town.

"Kenny, what did ya'll decide to do? You going to stay?"

"No. You know how low our house is. We're going to get off the island. In fact, we're leaving first thing in the morning."

"Don't blame you. You going into the Cape?"

"Yeah. We're going to one of the houses there that I was telling you about."

"Is that going to be high enough," I asked. "That area's there is not much higher than it is here."

"Janice has done some research on the web. The houses that we have access to are three or four feet higher than here."

"Three or four feet could be important."

"What are you and Jill going to do?" Kenny asked.

"I want to leave, but Jill is still on the fence. What are Doc and Peggy doing?"

"They left today. Caught a plane to Boston. Going to stay with their kids."

At that time, Rucker, and his wife, Lillian, walked in, and came over to our table.

"Hey, guys. Have a seat."

"Thanks. Are you guys all buttoned up now?"Rucker enquired.

"Yeah," we both answered at the same time. How about ya'll?"

"We're good. Just got a few last little things to finish up."

"So, Rucker," I asked, "Are ya'll going to stay?"

"Yeah. We've decided to stay. Our neighbor across the canal has a new three story concrete house. It's built to the new hurricane code. We're going to stay with them."

"You know, the storm surge could still be bad," I cautioned. You sure ya'll really want to do that?"

"Yeah. You know, I was here for Charlie, and I rode that one out okay. So, I think we'll be alright. Besides, Lillian's never been in a storm before. It's always been on her bucket list to go through one with me. We've always done everything together- we figure that we ought to do this together, too. You know- a 'Riders on the Storm' kind of thing. And, if we do get blown away, at least we'll go out together. Besides, when things get dangerous Lillian tends to get a little excited- if you know what I mean."

Kenny interrupted, "Damn. Rucker, you're just a dirty old man. You're planning to get in your wife's pants in the middle of the storm, aren't you?"

"So- I've got a bucket list, too! Now, what are ya'll drinking? I'll buy us a pitcher.

Just after Rucker left for the bar, Jill returned from having made her rounds checking with friends and neighbors. She looked worried.

"Hey, Babe," I greeted her. "What's up?"

"We're in trouble guys. Have ya'll seen the latest NHC forecast?"

"Nope. What are they showing now?"

"Here, take a look!"

She punched up the screen on her smart phone which displayed the most recent forecast cone. The wedge was no longer anchored on the east coast. Rather, the storm was now projected to come up the state's west coast, with the track of the storm forecast to pass directly over St James City."

We passed the phone around, each in turn staring at the screen, mentally processing the details, and implications, of what we were seeing. We all understood that this news wasn't good. Our little town, and all of us in it, was in serious trouble.

"Kenny, Jill and I will be coming over tomorrow afternoon to stay with ya'll in Cape Coral. If you want I can bring my generator, gas, charcoal grill, ice, and our food and supplies. I've got a couple of extra couple of bottles of whisky, too."

"Sounds good, Jim. And, please, make sure you bring that whisky. I suspect that we're going to need it. Rucker, ya'll are welcome to come, too. We have plenty of room."

"Appreciate the offer, Kenny. I really do. But, Lillian and I are serious about staying here. I still think that we'll be okay."

After that no one had much else to say. I suspect we were all wondering the same thing. What was going to happen to our precious little town? And, would we ever be able to drink a beer together again?

Chapter Six

Monday, September 11, 2017- St. James City, Florida

"We got lucky!"

Kenny had just said what we all knew to be the truth. At 7:35 the previous night Irma had jogged slightly to the right of its forecasted path, and had come ashore at Marco Island-roughly 50 miles to the south of St. James City. That unexpected deviation saved our island. The storm's path took it slightly to the east of Ft. Myers, and from there on into the heart of Central Florida. Those there took a fearsome pounding. The roofs of many houses, trees, power lines were all badly damaged, and wide swaths of the county were inundated by severe flooding. It would take weeks before power could be restored to the most heavily impacted regions, and months before some of the lowest lying areas would dry out. Irma had been a mighty storm.

But, in St. James City, we had indeed gotten lucky. Because the storm had passed to our east we had been on the weak side of the hurricane. And critically, because of this path, the strongest winds had blown offshore. Consequently, we avoided storm surge altogether. In fact, the opposite had occurred- the bottoms of many of our bayous and canals became exposed as water was pushed out into the Gulf. A lot of trees were damaged on the island, and some folks' houses were missing things like siding, tiles, shutters, or pool screens- but, by and large, with the exception of a few seawalls that had collapsed due to the extremely low water, the island had been spared significant damage.

We'd driven back on to the island as soon as we'd cleaned and buttoned up the borrowed Cape Coral house where we'd ridden out the storm. We were delighted, and surprised, that we'd been able to get back onto the island this quickly. We had all heard the many horror stories about how long it had taken folks to get back on the island after Hurricane Charlie in 2004. But, as we drove into Matlacha we instantly understood that no guards being posted at the foot of the Matlacha Bridge meant that our island must have been spared.

The first thing folks did when they returned to the island was, of course, to check out their own houses for damage. In our case, we had lost the siding from the east side of our third story, and our yard was covered in limbs blown off the many trees that surround the house. But, that, and no power, was the extent of our damage. Shortly, I had our generator running- and we were back in business- so to speak. We'd been lucky indeed.

The next thing that most folks did was to check on their friends' houses. Because many people had evacuated out of state and were having to rely on sensationalistic network news coverage for information, they were worried sick about the state of their property. It felt good to be able to call them and report that the damage wasn't nearly as severe as they'd assumed.

Kenny and I rode together to check on Doc's house. We had been very worried about his big fishing boat he'd left hanging on his lift. We'd helped to tie the boat down as well as we could, but we both knew that the windage of that much hull size, combined with the weight of the boat, when exposed to the force of winds in excess of 100 miles per hour, could have done significant damage. But, as we drove into his yard, we were delighted to see that the boat was hanging exactly as we'd left it- not damaged at all. In fact, as we surveyed his property the only damaged we could see were a few fronds missing off the top of his tiki hut, and the side door on the east side of his garage was standing open, looking as if it must have blown in. When we looked into the garage through that open door we could see that a lot of stuff had gotten wet from the rain, but otherwise, we couldn't see much damage. I appeared that the casing around the door frame had splintered, but we knew that that could be easily repaired, and repainted. We were delighted that Doc's stuff had survived the storm largely unscathed. And Doc, when Kenny called to report this information, was delighted, too. After getting this report he relayed that he and Peggy would fly back home as soon as the airports were re-opened.

Chapter Seven

It had taken us a week to prepare for the storm's arrival. It took about that much time to get all of those preparations undone, and at least that much time to repair whatever damage had been done. The days passed in a whirl of activity- everyone wanting to get their own stuff fixed, but helping friends and neighbors, too, as they needed assistance. At night, because the bars and restaurants hadn't yet- due to a lack of electricity- reopened- - we gathered at each other's homes- to share meals, drinks, and stories. And, there were no shortage of tales to tell, as everyone who'd ridden out the storm had something of interest to pass along, and those that hadn't wanted to hear all about what they'd missed. And, in some fundamental way we were just pleased that we'd survived to be together again. The days' work was hard, and, of course, we missed having air conditioning, but still- looking back on it- those days were actually kind of fun.

Doc and Peggy had finally been able to fly-in four days after the storm had passed. We were all glad that they were finally home. Since I expected him to be busy for a few days getting all of his stuff back in order I was a little surprised when Doc called me the next morning.

"Good morning, Jim. You up and about?"

"Yeah. I'm kicking. What's happening? Ya'll need some help over there?"

"Not really, Jim. But, I was wondering if you could come over and take a look at something. I know that you've got a penchant for solving mysteries, and I've got something here I'd like to get your thoughts about."

I laughed. "A mystery, huh? I don't know that I've got penchant for them. I think I've just gotten lucky a few times. But, I'll be glad to come over. Now a good time?"

"Yeah. I'll meet you at my garage door."

I finished the cup of tea that I'd been sipping, and went upstairs to tell Jill where I was going.

"Hey, Babe," I said. "Doc called and wants me to come over to his house to take a look at something. He said it's some kind of mystery."

"Oh, crap! Not again. Don't tell me that somebody's dead?"

"Oh, no! I don't think it's anything like that- he didn't sound upset. I think he just wants a second opinion. It's probably just a plumbing problem, or an issue on his boat, or something like that."

I could understand Jill's reaction. After having relocated to St. James City we had managed to become involved, through no fault or effort of our own, in helping to resolve- mostly through dumb luck- four different, unrelated, homicides that had taken place on the island. In each case one, or both, of us had come close to losing our own lives. This type of thing was nothing that we ever wanted to become entangled in again.

As I drove my pick-up truck the dozen or so blocks to his house at the corner of Emerald and Warren I reflected back on those previous episodes. Jill didn't have to worry- there was no way that I wanted to ever again find myself in that position. As I neared his house, I could see him standing near the side door to his garage. He waved me to pull the truck into the yard on that side of his house.

After I walked up, and shook his hand, he asked: "Jim, take a look at this door frame, and tell me what you think?"

"The storm blew it in, Doc. Don't you remember Kenny telling you about that?"

"Yeah, I remember. But, after I looked at this damage a little closer I'm not so sure that's what happened. That's why I want your opinion. Take a closer look, and tell me what you see."

I took my glasses off, and bent over to inspect the frame surrounding the inside-opening door. I knew that the house had been built during the building boom of the 1980's, and consequently, had not been subject to the State's strengthened post- Hurricane Andrew building codes. I also suspected that the builder back in those days had probably used the cheapest grade of lumber he could find when the house had been quickly thrown together. Therefore, I was expecting to see that the inside edge of the frame was splintered where the wind-pounded door had battered the metal latch out of the door jamb. I'd had enough problems with wallowed-out screw holes giving up the ghost in my own old house to have expected anything else. But, when I looked, that was not what I found.

Instead, I could see that the strike plate was still firmly attached, and the inside edge of the jamb was intact. And, I was surprised to see that what was damaged was the outside area surrounding the latch- both on the door and the frame itself. It simply appeared as if someone had used a pry bar of some sort to open the door. I studied the damage for several additional minutes- going through the mental analysis process one more time- before I gave Doc my opinion. I slowly straightened up, put my glasses back on, looked him in the eye, and said:

"Doc, it looks to me like you've probably been broken into. Are you missing anything?"

"That's what I thought, too. And, yeah, I am. But, it's kind of funny, the only thing I'm missing is that old chart that Ernie, gave me. But, that doesn't make much sense, does it? Why would someone break into my house in the middle of a hurricane to steal only that? All it had on it were some stupid fishing numbers- and at this point we don't even know how many of those spots were even any good. That doesn't make any sense to me."

"I don't know, Doc," I laughed. "But, those few spots we did fish off that chart worked pretty well, if you remember. I've got tell you Doc," I said with a glint in my eye, "I'm pretty mad now that you lost all those other spots before we even got to fish them."

"But, I didn't lose them," Doc said. "I put them all in my chart plotter as soon as Ernie gave me that old chart- just so I'd have them when we went fishing."

"Wow! That's a relief," I said. "So, no harm, no foul?"

"I guess," Doc replied hesitantly. "But, something just doesn't feel right about this. And, I sure don't want to have to tell Ernie that someone stole his chart right after he gave it to me.

"Yeah," I agreed. "I bet he'll be pissed that you lost that chart. Are you going to report this to the Sheriff's office?"

"I hadn't thought about that," Doc said. "Do you think I should? There really wasn't much damage, or anything."

"Yeah. But, I probably would- just to be safe. Hang on a minute and let me get my phone out of the truck, and I'll give you the name and number of the Sheriff's detective who's responsible for the island. He and I know each other. He's a good guy."

I returned quickly, and gave Doc the direct phone number for Lieutenant Mike Collins. I suggested that Doc let me know when he was scheduled to meet with Collins, and I'd come over to make an introduction. With that, I said goodbye, and drove home, thinking about how glad I was that Doc had not lost the coordinates for all those grouper holes.

Chapter Eight

The next morning, my phone rang. It was Doc.

"Good morning, Jim, if you've got some time this morning, Lieutenant Collins is coming over at 11:00; and after that I've arranged for you and me to meet Ernie for lunch. Can you make it?"

"Can do. I'll be over at eleven."

I arrived a little early since I wanted to be able to surprise Collins. He'd been the lead investigator in the four previous murder cases in which we'd played a role. I was actually looking forward (in a slightly sadistic sort of way) to seeing the look on the Lieutenant's face when he discovered that once again I was involved in one of his cases. I didn't expect, given the difficulties and embarrassments that those previous cases had caused him, that the look would be a smile. Truthfully, I didn't know what how he might react. I just hoped that he wouldn't shoot me when I said hello! I hid in the garage as he drove up.

"Mr. McLaughlin?" Collins asked as he walked towards the garage door where Doc was standing.

"That's me," Doc replied. "I really appreciate you coming out to take a look at this. I hate to bother you over something this trivial, but I thought maybe it would be best if I reported it."

"Not a problem," Collins answered. "I told you yesterday that I'd be glad to come over. But, I am curious about how you got my direct number? Usually, when someone has a problem, they call the Department, and a dispatcher will determine who should respond. Normally, in a case like this they would have just have sent one of the patrol deputies assigned to the island to come over make a report."

"Well, I hope that I haven't caused a problem," Doc said. A friend of mine gave me your number. But, if you'd prefer to call in a deputy, I'll certainly understand."

"A friend?" Collins asked.

I, of course, had been listening to the whole conversation and decided that now would be as good a time as any to make my appearance. I stuck my head out of the door and said, "How are you doing, Mike?"

Collins' face froze. An almost dazed look appeared in his eyes, a glaze which slowly transitioned into an expression that could have passed for confusion, anger, fear, or all three. Throughout it all his mouth hung half open- giving the impression that he had been rendered speechless. I had just decided to repeat my greeting, but before I could get the words out of my mouth, Collins recovered. I got the distinct feeling that he then retreated behind a cloak of professionalism- probably to disguise whatever it was that he was truly feeling.

"Hello, Jim. You, I suppose, would be the 'friend' who gave my private, unlisted, number to Mr. McLaughlin?"

"Yes, of course. I wanted my good friend Doc to have access to the very cream of the crop among the Lee County Sheriff Department's investigators. I hoped I haven't caused a problem?"

Collins opened his mouth, as if to reply, but quickly shut it. I guessed that he had planned to say something along the lines of "the only problem I have is you, Story." But, he had obviously backtracked from that impulse.

Instead, in a more politically correct manner, he said: "Not a problem at all, Jim. As a servant of the people in Lee County, I am here to protect and serve, and today I am happy to be here to serve Mr. McLaughlin." Turning away from me, and facing directly at Doc, he began again: "Sir, you indicated on the phone that your house at been burglarized during the hurricane?"

"Yes, Sir. I believe that it was."

"I guess we shouldn't be surprised by that. There is always a bit of looting immediately after a hurricane. Folks need a lot of stuff then. But, I am surprised that there was looting in St. James City. This just doesn't seem like the kind of place for that to happen. But, I guess the times are changing. Now, Mr. McLaughlin, what do you believe was looted?"

"Mike," I began to say. "I don't believe that this was loo........."

Lieutenant Collins stopped me with a wave of his hand, a gesture quickly followed by an instruction to please not interrupt his interrogation again. I gave him an apologetic, quick hands-up gesture to indicate my capitulation to his wishes, and took a half step backwards to signal my complete compliance.

"Now, Mr. McLaughlin, again, what do you believe was looted?

"Inspector," Doc replied, "with all due respect, I don't believe that this was a case of looting."

We could see Collins flinch and stiffen his spine, but, still, he did back down. "Okay, Mr. McLaughlin, we'll do this your way. Now, what do you believe was taken in this burglary that wasn't a likely episode of post-hurricane looting?"

"It was just an old fishing chart, sir?"

"A fishing chart? You mean like a map, or something?" Then looking purposefully in my direction, he asked: "It wasn't a pirate map, was it?"

"No," Doc said. "This was a modern type of navigation chart. A chart, as I'm sure you know, is, in fact, a kind of map- a map of the sea used for marine piloting. To be precise, sir, this was a '1977 edition of NOAA National Ocean Service, C&GS 1113, chart number 11140- Habana to Tampa Bay.' Soundings on the chart are in fathoms."

"What's a fathom?" Collins asked.

"One fathom is equal to six feet of depth," Doc replied.

"Okay." Collins responded. "Was there anything special, or noteworthy about this particular chart?"

"No, it was just a beautiful, old-style government chart. It featured a bright yellow color for land areas, and the sea featured various shades of blue and gray. For some reason they don't use those colors on charts anymore." Doc responded.

"And, you are certain that nothing else was taken?"

"I am positive. I have carefully inventoried all my other charts. None of them were taken. It was just that one."

At that I saw Collins rub his chin. From our previous encounters I thought that this meant he was reconsidering his previous position. I was soon proved right.

"Mr. McLaughlin, I apologize. You are right, this doesn't sound like a case of hurricane looting to me. It seems more like a targeted theft. Was this chart valuable? "

I guess it probably might be worth something. Any old chart has some value as a collector's item- maybe 25 bucks. But, this one was far from pristine. It had been stained by sea water, had been folded and unfolded so many times that it was near tearing. And, it had some silly writing on the back- for some reason someone had penciled in "A Dummies Guide to Household Repairs." The surface of the chart was also covered in inked-in notations of grouper holes. I guess those numbers might be worth something to a grouper fisherman, but the chart was so old it'd be hard to say if those marks were still any good. And, besides, I didn't buy the chart. It was given to me a couple of months back by a friend here on the island. I'm at a loss as to why anyone might want to steal it. It can't be worth much because it's so easy and cheap these days to order reprints of any old chart. "

With that explanation I could see Collins bow his head slightly and rub his eyes. After doing this for a few seconds, he looked up, stared at me with what might have been a slightly exasperated expression, and said: "Story- I don't want you to take what I'm about to say to you in the wrong way- because, truly, I think a lot of you, and, of course, I think even more of your wife. But, why do you think it is that every time I run into you, you get me involved in some weird, convoluted, twisted, irrational, likely-to-get-me-fired, impossible-to- make-sense-of mess?   I go for months, even years, at a time, and have no cases to solve more complicated than some druggy swiping something to sell for cash, or some jilted husband stabbing his hot-to- trot wife's back-door lover. But, then, out of the blue, my phone rings, and it's you- and then my logical, well-ordered, organized life goes to hell. I'd sworn that if I ever saw your name on my caller ID again I'd refuse to answer the phone. But, now you've even gotten someone else making your calls for you. So- what am I to do? Maybe I'll just give up, go ahead, and retire. I don't think that I've got it in me to spend months trying to make sense of another one of the damn puzzles that seem to attach themselves to you."

With that he stopped, held his palms up to indicate that his outburst was over, turned back towards Doc, and said: "Mr. McLaughlin, I apologize for my behavior. It's just that I'm overcome with emotion at once again seeing my old friend, Jim Story. Now, let's step inside the garage. I'd like to see where and how these charts were stored.

Once inside Doc pointed at a several chart tubes sitting on a shelf on a storage rack against the garage's wall.

"That's where the chart was," Doc told Collins.

"How'd you know that it was missing?" he asked.

"Like I said, this chart had recently been given to me. Therefore, it was on top, and, besides, the color of the old tube it came in was dark blue. All the others I have are gray. So, it was quickly pretty obvious to me that it was missing."

"I see that the other chart tubes are all labeled. Was the missing chart labeled, too?" Collins asked.

"Yeah. I'm kind of fastidious about my charts. I'd put a label on the bottom- '1977-Habana to Tampa Bay-Ernie.' Ernie is the name of the guy that gave me the chart."

"That wouldn't by any chance be Ernie Valdez?" Collins asked.

"Yes, it was," Doc replied. "Do you know him?"

"Actually, this is now starting to get more interesting. I was at Mr. Valdez' house this morning. Someone broke into his house during the hurricane, too. But, strangely enough- nothing there seemed to be missing."

"Mike," I said, "that's just too weird to be coincidental."

"Jim, I have to agree with that assessment. Now, Mr. McLaughlin, do these other charts in the racks also have good grouper numbers on them?"

"Sure."

"So, we have to conclude that this burglary wasn't about just stealing grouper numbers. In other words, someone was after that specific chart. Do you have any idea why someone might want it?"

"Not a clue."

Then the Lieutenant's phone buzzed. He excused himself, stepped away and answered it. When he came back he said:

"Mr. McLaughlin, I am sorry about the loss of your chart, and the damage to your door. I'll have a technical team here in an hour to dust for prints. And, I'll keep you posted on any progress we make. I'll put the word out for our guys to be on the lookout for this specific chart. We'll check the pawn shops, and troll the internet. But, sir, I will advise you that these types of random cases of loo...- excuse me- random cases of theft, are extremely difficult to resolve. Let me know if you think of anything else that might be relevant. Now, I've got to be going- somebody just stole an outboard boat motor up in Matlacha.

As Collins turned to leave, he looked again in my direction, and said: "Jim, I'm sorry about giving you a hard time. I was just scared you were going to dump another damn body on me. You don't have one, do you?"

"Nope. No bodies this time."

"Good. Please give my best to Jill."

I nodded, and as he walked away I almost felt sorry for him. I knew that there was a lot of truth to what he'd said about our previous interactions. And, besides- I owed that man a lot. Not only had he saved my life, but more importantly, he'd saved Jill's life, too.

Chapter Nine

Doc had arranged for us to meet Ernie for lunch at his house on the north end of the island. When Doc had told him that we were going to bring him some grouper filets Ernie had suggested that we grill them in his backyard. All we had to bring was the fish. Ernie would provide everything else.

Ernie's house was off a side road that ran to the west of Stringfellow. It was a small, neat cottage, almost hidden under a grove of shady tropical trees. As we pulled into the drive way we could see Ernie tending an old fashioned outdoor grill. I guess that I had been expecting to see a Weber, or something like that. But, instead, Ernie was tending coals that smoldered under a heavy metal grate that nestled on brackets inside three simple poured cement walls- definitely 'old school.' I hadn't eaten food cooked on a grill like that in a very long time. From the smoke stains on the walls, and the well worn bare dirt surrounding the grill, I guessed that Ernie cooked out here often.

As we walked towards him, Ernie wiped his hands on a clean white cotton towel draped over his shoulder and stepped out to greet us. I guess that I had been expecting Ernie to be small, frail, and shriveled- an old man nearing the end of his days. But, my guess would have been wrong. Clearly, Ernie was old. And, from the gaunt hollows in his cheeks, and the shadows under his eyes, I could see that cancer had begun to take its toll. But, other than that, he was still an impressive, almost imposing, figure. Despite the ravages of time he stood at least 6'3", with a frame very much like that of an athlete- he was rangy, strong, straight, balanced, and well-proportioned. I didn't detect an ounce of fat. But, despite his impressive figure the most striking features of the man were his hazel eyes- eyes one could tell had seen more than most. His pupils were clear and bright, and his gaze, somehow, seemed both cool, and quiet. I've always felt that eyes were indeed the windows into a man's soul, and his managed to convey, not so much traditional intelligence but rather, a sense of alert awareness- eyes able to faultlessly analyze and decipher situations and persons that confronted him. I wasn't surprised, as I approached, that he didn't have to spend a lot of time looking at me to form an opinion.

But, whatever wariness his eyes may have initially conveyed, as we grew nearer, that quickly disappeared. The cautious look that I had initially detected on his handsome face had now dissolved into a genuine smile, a welcoming expression that now spread across his entire face. He warmly embraced Doc, before turning to offer me his large, strong hand to shake.

"Mr. Story," he said. "It is indeed an honor to meet you. Over the past several years I have heard much about how you have managed to assist our Sheriff's Department."

"Thank you for your kind words, Mister Valdez, but I assure you that it was more a case of the Sheriff assisting me, than the other way around. Regardless, I am honored to meet you as well."

With those words, we both dipped our heads slightly - unconsciously having adopted some kind of archaic display of mutual respect. With these ceremonies out of the way, Ernie directed us towards the chairs and table that he had arranged under the trees beyond the hot grill.

"Doctor McLaughlin," Ernie asked politely, "does the bag in your hand contain the fish filets about which we spoke earlier?"

"Indeed it does, Sir. And, that is why we are here. We caught these fish using the numbers you provided. We want you to share them with you to thank you for having done that."

"I appreciate the sentiment, Doc, but I assure you, no thanks are required. As I told you before, I wanted you, for a variety of reasons, to have that chart. Now, give me the bag, and I'll put the filets on ice. And, please, have a seat at the table. We should talk some before we begin to eat. Would you like a beer? I'm afraid that all I have is American 'Hatuey.' It, of course, is not as good as when it was brewed in Cuba; but at least, it still reminds me of home."

Doc and I both quickly responded that we would enjoy drinking a beer.

"Mr. Valdez," I began, "when ....."

He interrupted me. "Please, we are now friends. You may call me Ernie. May I call you Jim?"

"Of course, sir, and Ernie it is. Now, if you don't mind me asking, I was wondering when did you leave Cuba, and when did you come to the States?"

"Jim, I don't at all mind you asking. These events have, of course, defined my life in so many ways. My family and I left Cuba in 1959. Initially, we went to Puerto Rico. But, shortly after that I came to Miami to live with a friend- a friend whose family had also left Cuba."

"Those must have been difficult times."

"Yes, Jim. They were very difficult times. But, as I'm suspect you know, we Cubans are a hard working, industrious people. Most who came over then were able to survive, and many have been able to do well."

"Indeed," I said with a smile. "Ya'll own Miami now."

Ernie laughed, and replied "Indeed we do, and, not just Miami, you know?"

"I know," returning the laugh.

"Ernie, now that tourism and travel to Cuba are once again being allowed do you plan to return there?"

"Jim, I would love to. But, until I can stand in the middle of the Plaza de la Revolution and yell loudly 'Castro Sucks,' I don't want to go back. And, with what's facing me, it doesn't look like I'll ever have that opportunity. But, for the time being, enough about Cuba- we can talk about that later. While you and the Doctor continue to enjoy your beers, let me work on lunch."

We, of course, agreed. As Ernie seasoned and oiled the fish I could see that he had already prepared a skillet of sautéed ripe plantains, and a pot of, what I presumed to be from its smell, 'congri' (Cuba's ubiquitous combination of simultaneously cooked rice and beans). A few moments later, armed with fresh beers from the cooler, we sat down to enjoy this traditional Cuban fisherman's meal. I was honored that Ernie had thought enough of our angling skills to have prepared it for us. When we were through, he returned to the grill and prepared Cuban coffee in a small silver 'moka' pot. When the aromatic espresso was ready he poured a serving onto the sugar that waited in each of three tiny cups and stirred. Now, it was time to talk.

Chapter Ten

On the drive north, Doc and I had agreed to delay telling Ernie about the theft of the chart until we felt the time was right. I, of course, planned to leave the decision about when that time was to Doc. He, I knew, was concerned that Ernie would probably be upset about him having lost this cherished document only a few days after it had been given to him. And, the fact that Ernie, too, had recently been burglarized only complicated the matter. I was curious about how, and when, Doc planned to bring the subject up. Apparently, Doc decided that the rapturous period that followed our first sips of that thick, aromatic bittersweet espresso was as good a time as any to come clean.

As we all savored the lingering taste in our mouths, Doc spoke: "Ernie, my home was burglarized during the hurricane. It appears that someone broke into my locked garage. But, surprisingly, all that the thief wanted was the chart that you gave me. It is now missing. But, fortunately, before it was stolen I had entered most of the coordinates of the marked fishing spots into my GPS. I want to apologize to you for having lost this chart. I know that it meant a lot to you, and, because of that, it also meant a lot to me. I am sorry."

After Doc confessed, Ernie stared, for just a moment, directly at him. No expression was visible- neither on his face, nor in his eyes. To me it looked as if I was seeing the face of a man not unused to having to deal with the unexpected. I felt that what I was seeing was the face of a man that had always been able to instantly plot the proper response to any such challenge- an appropriate response not unduly burdened by sentiment, or morals, but rather guided chiefly by effectiveness, and expediency. I seemed to sense in Ernie's expression that that ability may have been honed to a fine edge by a lifetime where the consequences of such decisions may have meant death, or survival. But, in that same instant, I had a sense, possibly from glimpsing what I took to be unexpected empathy in his eyes that for him the balance of those consequences had now somehow fundamentally shifted. I guessed that knowing you only have a short time left to live could do to that to a man. Given these impressions, I was curious about how Ernie would respond to Doc's news.

"Doc," Ernie began, "Really, I am not all that surprised by what you have told me, and frankly, I am now glad that the damn chart was stolen- at least glad that it was stolen without you or your wife being harmed. I have been worried that my having given it to you might have put you in harm's way. That, at least, is no longer on my conscience."

"Ernie, why were you not surprised? And, why would an old chart have put us in harm's way?"

"Doc, I am an old man. During my long lifetime I have, as men sometimes will, made enemies. I, too, was burglarized during the storm. But, in my case, nothing was taken. And, now I know that they were looking for the chart that I gave to you. For the last ten years, after my wife died, I have lived in this house alone. Perhaps, I'm finally starting to get soft, or senile. None of us, I suspect, want to die without having left a record of our proudest achievement, without some evidence to show that we actually were here and that what we did mattered. I wanted you to have that chart- not only because of the many grouper numbers on it, but also because of a something else, a little challenge, that I included on it. But, enough about that damn chart- I'm glad that you were able to catch fish using it, and I'm glad that you weren't hurt when it was stolen. But, trust me, the loss of that chart is not important- either to me, or to you. We really should never speak of it again. Jim, tell me, how did you come to the island?"

With that it was obvious that the subject had been changed. I answered his question, and then turned the tables on him. "Ernie, how did you come to the island?"

"My wife and I moved to Pine Island twenty years ago, shortly after we had sold our boat building business, and retired."

"Ernie, tell me about your business?"

"I had received my degree in Marine Design from the University of Havana. After I came to the states I was eventually able to use that knowledge to help others who were building boats. Back then, given the advent of using fiberglass to create inexpensive hulls, and the rapid development of outboard engines, almost everyone wanted to get into the boat building business. I guess then it seemed like a quick way to get rich. But, almost none of them actually knew how to go about building a decent boat. I was just in the right place, at the right time. Many, if not most, of the hulls from that era came out of molds that I produced. As a consequence, my marine consulting business flourished. I made a great deal of money, and was able to travel much of the world on business. But, then I got old, sold the business, and we moved here."

"Why here?" I asked. I was expecting him to answer with the same platitudes about the beauty of the island and the quiet lifestyle here that we all use when asked the same question. I was certainly not expecting the answer that he gave.

"Because, I wanted to be near Useppa Island."

I looked at him with a puzzled expression, before saying, "Why Useppa?"

"As I told you earlier, shortly after I left Cuba I came to Miami from Puerto Rico to stay with my friend. What I didn't tell you was that I came because he had told me that he was being recruited by the C.I.A to serve in a group being formed to invade Cuba and overthrow Castro. He and I both wanted to be part of that. After a few weeks of interviews we were both selected. We were beyond honored to be among the very first of our brothers chosen. One night we came to a house on Calle Ocho for a meeting- everything then was always arranged secretively, we had been warned to never tell anyone, not even our families, about these meetings. But, this, as it turned out, was not an ordinary meeting. The guys at the house, we assumed that they were all from the C.I.A., told us that we would not be going home that night. Instead, we were told that we would be leaving from that house to go on a secret mission. Several hours later, after the sky had gotten dark, I think that it was nearly eleven o'clock, my friend Juan and I were told to go use the bathroom. Then, when we came out, we were blindfolded, put into the back seat of a car, and advised to just try to get some sleep. They explained that we were going to be driven to a training area for the invasion force, and that, for reasons of maintaining secrecy about the base's location, the car would not be stopping, for any reason, until we reached our destination. Juan and I, of course, were excited to have finally actually become a part of the fight against Castro. Immediately we began to ask the guys in the car, despite having just heard their warning concerning the need for secrecy, about where we were heading. We were calmly told that they couldn't tell us, and, furthermore were informed that if we attempted to remove our blindfolds to look outside the car to determine where we were going that we would be shot. They then told us that our bodies would be dumped into the Everglades for the alligators to eat. Given the way that they said that, I believed them. The next time I removed my blindfold, only after having been instructed to do so by my CIA handler, I was standing on, what I learned much later, was Useppa Island. Juan and I had been selected to possibly become part of what eventually became known as Brigada Asalto 2506!"

Doc and I both exclaimed at the same time- "You trained on Useppa for the Bay of Pigs invasion?"

Chapter Eleven

"Ernie!" I exclaimed. "That is amazing. I would like to hear all about that."

"Jim," Ernie replied, I would love to share this story with you. But, not, I'm afraid, today. I am no longer as strong as I once was. Preparing for your visit, cooking our meal, and talking has worn me out. Perhaps we can get together again soon, and talk then about those long ago times."

"I'm so sorry, Ernie," Doc interrupted as he stood up. "We didn't mean to overstay our welcome. Let us help you clean up the dishes, and we will then leave so you can get some rest."

"That would be kind, Doc. Let us do that. But, before you go can we schedule a time for us to get together again- soon. I have very much enjoyed being with you."

"What about the same time one week from now?" I asked both Doc and Ernie.

"That would be fine with me," Ernie replied. "Doc?"

"Absolutely- I look forward to it. Can we bring more grouper when we come?"

"Of course, if you like," Ernie replied. "But, I was wondering if, instead, you might have any snapper that you could bring? I have a very fine traditional Cuban snapper recipe that I would like to prepare for you."

I was delighted with Ernie's request. I knew that, if there was one thing that Doc had plenty of in his freezer, it was snapper. At least he had lots of Mangrove, Lane, and Yellow Tails. I knew he also had a fair amount of delicious Vermillion Snapper. These species were readily available offshore- and was what Doc and his friends usually fished for after the day's grouper limit was filled.

But, I was hoping that Ernie wasn't asking for filets of American Red Snapper since, given the restrictions on fishing for this variety, the freezer might not be so accommodating.

"Ernie- of course I have snapper in my freezer. What variety would you like?"

"It doesn't really matter that much. But, Mangrove, or Yellow Tail, would be the most traditional."

I could see Doc's face brighten before replying, "Ernie, I look forward to returning next week with all the snapper filets that we can eat. Now let us help you finish cleaning up."

Shortly the table, grill, and cooler were all cleaned and made ready for their next usage. The dishes were stacked. I helped Ernie carry them along with the pans and cooking equipment back into his house. As I entered through the back door to the kitchen I was immediately struck by how neatly organized it was. For example, on one wall was a rack that held dozens and dozens of spice containers- I couldn't help but note that these bottles were arranged in precise alphabetical order. I looked into the pantry cupboard as Ernie opened its door to return several items to it. Each shelf I noticed was neatly labeled, and the cans organized in neat rows. Ernie washed everything by hand in the sink. I dried, smiling as I did thinking back to how my grandmother used to make me do this for her. When everything had been washed and dried I handed the pans to Ernie as he returned them to their cabinet for storage. Again, I could see neatness and organization. I made a note to myself to never let Ernie, should he come to our house for dinner, see the inside of our kitchen cabinets.

Once everything was properly stored we rejoined Doc outside. Then he and I shook Ernie's hand, and fondly said good bye.

As soon as we were in Doc's car, heading south on Stringfellow Road, we began talking about the visit.

"Doc," I said, "I really enjoyed meeting Ernie. What an interesting man! I can't wait to learning more about when he was on Useppa Island, and about what happened after that."

"Me, too," Doc replied. "You know, don't you, that the guys the CIA trained there became the leadership cadre for the Bay of Pigs invasion?"

"Truthfully," I answered, "I only know that some people were trained there. I really don't know all that much about who they were, or what they did. But, I'm really looking forward to seeing him again and learning more. In the meantime, I think I'll do some research on the subject."

"Well, I hope you don't have so much research in mind that you won't be able to go fishing!"

"Doc, there's no risk of that. When do you have in mind?"

"I was thinking about going out the day after tomorrow. Kenny told me he would be available. How's that work for you?"

"My calendar's wide open. But, why don't you hold on while I check the marine forecast? You know how I am- before I commit, let me Google the weather."

"Jim, you've got the queasiest stomach of anybody I know. But, go ahead pull it up, and let me know what it says."

A minute later I responded, "We're good. Five to ten winds out of the Southeast; seas one to two feet. You can't do better than that. What time you want to leave?"

"Let's make it six. That okay with you?"

"Perfect!"

Chapter Twelve

The morning promised to dawn still, and bright. The first thing I do every morning in Southwest Florida is to look into the sky-just to see if there are any storms nearby. But, this morning the only clouds visible were just a few distant soft cumulus billows far off to the east, innocent pink-tinged puffs still in the early formative stages of organizing for their explosive build-out over the Lake and the Glades.

I always marvel at the daily spectacle that takes place in Southwest Florida's late summer skies. I've learned to love the weather pattern in this part of the State- it is fascinating to observe each morning as the usual gentle east-southeasterly trades initiate the daily process by pushing moisture from the Atlantic onto the already water-logged southern end of the Florida peninsula. Then, as the day's hot sun rapidly warms up the land, and the water standing on much of it, moisture-laden air begins to be forced upwards. These drafts eventually develop into small clouds, and then they, and the heavy moisture they contain, rise even higher into the sky. All the while, the trade winds continue to slowly encourage these growing mountains of vapor to the west- adding even more moisture to the escalating towers as they slowly drift over the steaming Everglades. But later in the day, as the rapidly increasing heat of the land begins to suck a sea breeze out of the Gulf straight into the path of these advancing billows, the heavy but benign clouds start to become empowered. Trapped between winds from the east, and winds from the west, they become energized as they are forced even more rapidly upward, now the only direction left for them to move. As this process continues the resulting pillars of energy rise high into the sky- forty thousand feet, and even higher. Their tops becoming dark as the rising moisture embedded within them begins to condense as it encounters the cooler temperatures of the near stratosphere. This conflict eventually produces droplets of precipitation. These drops, as they grow larger, try to fall towards the ground- pulled downward by gravity- but still being pushed upwards by the hot air contained in the clouds. These opposing forces often cancel each other out causing the drops to fall, and then to rise, then to fall, and then to rise- the process repeated many, many times. And, each time, as the drops race upwards into the cold heavens, they freeze. This process, when repeated many times, depending upon the strength of the storm, forms ever larger crystals of ice. Eventually, once they become too heavy to continue to rise, and as the force within the clouds begins to dissipate, these particles fall to the ground as hail.

These battles between the conflicting forces of heat and gravity are not limited to just generating rain, or hail- these alternating forces also cause friction, in the process creating unimaginable quantities of static electricity. Eventually, these cloud-borne charges become so strong that they have to be released to the ground- i.e., as a lightning strike. This is the daily summertime process that makes Southwest Florida the lightning capital of the United States. In fact, the only part of the world with more lightning is Equatorial Africa. But, all of this activity is a mere prelude to the daily storm's crescendo. This final act is made possible as the heat within the storm is gradually lessened as the rays of the sun move lower, a development that allows the energy within the storm to be eventually overcome by the unrelenting coolness of the heavens. When this happens the air that has been rising all day is suddenly freed to rush back to earth- producing the strong storm force winds that always precede the rain. And, once the upward force of the rising hot air is dissipated, the water that has been transported upwards all day now has nothing to keep it airborne. The result is a familiar semi-tropical rainstorm. A deluge that is normally short in duration, but heavy in intensity. Then, only a few minutes after the rain begins, the daily storm drama is over- followed by a still, steaming humidity, and the welcome relative coolness that freshens and renews both the parched sands, and residents, of coastal Florida.

I knew, however, from looking at the morning's sky that today these storms would not develop until much later in the afternoon. In fact, the morning's conditions promised excellent fishing out in the Gulf. And, if all went according to plan, we should have our limit of fish, and be safely in port, well before the day's squalls reached their crescendos.

As usual, I was looking forward to the trip. I picked Kenny up, and we drove together to Doc's place. We were there at a quarter to six- there's nothing worse than being late to a free fishing trip. As usual, Doc was already on the boat, just finishing a few last minute details- buttoning the plastic windscreens out of the way, and stowing the food and beverages that his wife, Peggy, as usual, had provided.

"Morning, Doc!" Kenny enthused as we walked towards the boat, rods in hand and gear bags over our shoulders.

"Top of the morning to you, Kenny!" Doc replied- his normal sunny disposition evident already before the sun was even up. "Good morning to you, too, Jim."

"Good morning Doc," I replied. While I've always considered myself to be a morning person, somehow I think my response, when contrasted with Doc's more enthusiastic welcome, may have somehow seemed slightly surly. I hoped not. "Looks like we've got ourselves a great morning to go fishing!"

"That it does, Jim. That it does. I think we're going to limit out today!"

I laughed. "There's no question about it Doc! We always catch our limit when we go fishing with you."

"Come on, Jim. Don't put that kind of pressure on me. You know I don't handle pressure well."

"Don't hand me that nonsense. You know that you just thrive on the challenge of putting your friends on fish." I handed him my rods. "Do we have everything we need?"

"We need to stop outside the pass and catch bait, but otherwise we're good."

As we'd been talking I'd noticed that Kenny had already climbed onboard the boat and had rapidly stowed his gear. I smiled, knowing that this was just the normal manifestation of Kenny's usual "Let's get our asses in gear and go fishing" impatience. But, that was alright with me. I was anxious to get on the water, too. As soon as I gave Doc my gear bag I, too, climbed into the boat.

A minute later we were underway. Doc had done his customary job of expertly backing his big boat up, and quietly turning it around, in the narrow, boat-lined canal behind his house. By now there was enough reflective sunlight from the brightening eastern sky that we had no difficulty seeing our way out.

As soon as we had reached the channel, Doc turned the boat to the south. I knew that meant that we would be going out through San Carlos Bay- before heading towards the southwest for fishing. Since Doc usually prefers to fish by going to the north, and then heading due west out of Redfish Pass, I knew that he had not planned today's trip to be just a normal expedition. I had assumed my usual position alongside Doc at the leaning post.

As soon as the boat had settled onto a quiet plane I spoke: "Doc," I said, "it looks to me like we must be going out to explore some more of the numbers on Ernie's chart."

He looked over at me, and grinned. "Well, they worked out pretty good for us last time, didn't they?"

"I can't argue with that," I replied. "But, you've got hundreds of good spots on your charts already without having to go all the way down here. I think there may be more to it than that."

"Well, I'm not going to deny it, Jim. Ever since I heard Ernie say that there was a puzzle on that old chart I've been wondering what he meant. He said it like it was almost like a treasure map, or something. And, I've always been a sucker for Pirate stories. And, besides, if we can still catch fish at the same time that we are trying to solve a puzzle, what's the harm in that?"

I laughed. "Yeah, as long as we still catch fish!"

It was now Doc's turn to laugh.

"Do you have a particular spot in mind that you want to explore first?" I asked.

"Yeah, Jim, actually I do. But, why don't you take a look at the display and see if any of the locations stick out to you as needing to be explored?"

I positioned myself directly in front of the boat's large GPS chart display. I could see dozens of spots that Doc had loaded into the device along with their nomenclature. I alternated between scrolling the display to take a bigger scale look at the overall area, before focusing in for a closer more detailed inspection of each spot. When I did that I concentrated on the depth contours indicated on the chart. But, after five minutes of staring at the display I had only reached a couple of conclusions.

"Doc, it looks to me like some of the spots are too far inshore. I'm going to eliminate those. But, for the most part, the rest all look like they could hold promise. They are in deep enough water, and the bottom looks okay. For the most part the names all seem normal, too: 'Carlos' Grouper Hole;' 'Red Snapper I;' 'Javier's Sharks.' Nothing really stands out at me as unusual."

Doc stared in my eyes, and asked: "Nothing?"

"Well, not that much anyway. This is a stretch, I know. But, the only thing that stood out to me was the one spot that was marked with just an initial, and a number, 'B-26.' And, only then because the label's structure didn't match the way that all the other spots were named. But, if I had to pick one that's the one I would pick."

"Interesting," Doc said. "That's the one I picked, too. To solve a puzzle you've got to start somewhere."

"As long as we can catch some fish, too."

"There you go again, Jim. Putting pressure on the poor captain."

"Doc, you've never let me down, yet!"

Forty five minutes later Kenny roused himself from his deep slumber on top of a bean bag chair that he'd wedged in a corner against the transom. Those chairs do a remarkable job of smoothing the ride while supporting, and holding in place, a reclining fisherman on the long, often rough, runs far offshore. I knew from experience that he would be feeling well rested as he joined us at the helm.

"Good morning, again, Kenny," Doc said with a grin on his face. "You have a nice nap?"

"I sure did! I'm feeling great. Now, how long before we start fishing?"

"The GPS says we'll be there in twenty minutes," Doc replied.

"Where's 'there'?" Kenny asked. Are we going to one of that Cuban guy's holes again?"

"We sure are," Doc replied.

"Well, I hope it's better than the last one we fished," Kenny groused. "On the last one Jim caught all the fish. All I got was a danged shark."

"But, at least we got our limit of fish," Doc replied. "It's not my fault that you don't know how to fish!"

"Oh, come on, Doc. You know that I normally out fish both of you guys. I guess it just wasn't my day. But, why are we going to this spot? Did Ernie tell you that it's a good one?"

"Not exactly," Doc replied. "Jim and I just picked it off of the chart. We don't know if it's got fish, or not. It just looked interesting."

"Well, that certainly sounds encouraging!" Kenny said somewhat sarcastically. "I better go check to make sure my gear is ready."

Ten minutes later I heard Doc mumble to himself "Well, that doesn't look good."

"What is it, Doc," I replied. "Something wrong with the boat?"

"No. It's just that the radar shows there's another boat on top of the spot we're heading to. Go figure- here we are sixty miles out in the Gulf, we haven't seen another boat all morning, and when we finally get to where we want to fish, there's another boat already there."

I looked ahead of the boat in the direction we were pointing. "Yeah, I think I can see it up there. I can't be sure but it almost looks like it might be a sail boat. That seems kind of strange, doesn't it?"

"Sure does," Doc replied. "Usually guys don't bottom fish out of sail boats- the cockpits too small, the gunwales are too high, and they're just not laid out or equipped for fishing. Maybe they just stopped here for the night, and are going to be moving on shortly. We'll go up closer and take a look."

A few minutes later we approached the anchored vessel. I had been correct in identifying it as a sail boat. In this case, a sizeable sailing catamaran, probably about 40 to 45 feet in length. This particular type of boat is popular in South Florida and the Bahamas, primarily because of its shallow draft which allows it access to the thin waters of these coasts. It's also well liked because of the significant amount of space on board- usually multiple sleeping berths are contained in the twin hulls, while the main cabin contains the galley, dining, and living quarters between those structures. This large amount of living space makes these types of boats popular as rental options in the islands. It also makes them favorites for 'live-aboard' sailors. The biggest drawback to the design is the crafts' extreme width- a characteristic which makes finding suitable, secure, affordable dockage for these big boats a challenge. That, I suppose, is why St. James City has become home port to more than a few of these boats and their skippers. Kenny and I both, over the years, had become friends with several of these colorful nomadic characters. I had learned that these folks were often looking for any good excuse at night to get away from their lonely and claustrophobic cabins for a few hours- they could frequently be found sitting at the quiet end of the bars in town. Seldom, it seemed to me, did they want to participate in either the normal carryings on in the establishments, or to engage in in-depth conversation with the idolizing, curious, covetous tourists. I concluded that it just wasn't their natures. Essentially, most of them were loners- probably happiest when they were at sea; and slightly uncomfortable, and out of place, in a crowd. Which is not to say that they would ever turn down a free drink, or a free home cooked meal- especially one that had been prepared by one of the island's many accomplished female cooks. Many of these sea-going nomads, in some ways I thought relics of times gone by, had been frequent guests in all of our homes. Which is why, as we drew near, were able to recognize the boat anchored on top of our planned fishing spot.

Kenny spoke up first, "That looks like Jocko's boat."

"That's it okay," I answered. "That's the 'Lady Chatterley.' And, that's his dog, Bingo, sitting in the cockpit. I wonder if Jocko's onboard."

"Let's find out," Doc replied. He reached up and hit the button that activated the loud horn that sat on top of the boat's T-top. When that jarring sound had quieted, he yelled over: "Ahoy, Captain Jocko, are you on board?"

But, apart from Bingo raising his head in calm curiosity, there was no reply.

"That's strange," I said. "Why wouldn't he be on his boat all the way out here?"

"I don't think it's strange at all," Kenny answered. "Look what's hanging off the stern."

"You mean that boarding ladder?" I asked.

"Yeah. I don't know if you know this, but Jocko's an avid diver. I was talking with him one day when we were both at the barber shop down at the Center. I asked him if he liked to fish- you know I was going to try to pry some good grouper numbers out of him. But, he told me that he didn't really fish all that much. Instead, he told me that he spent most of his free time scuba diving. He said he was passionate about underwater archeology- especially as it related to the old Calusa villages. He said that he also liked looking for Spanish treasure, and stuff like that. So, my guess is, Jocko's just gone diving. Bingo's guarding the boat."

"But," Doc interjected, "why is he diving all the way out here? I would think this is way too far out for any Indian relics."

"Yeah. But, possibly, not too far out for treasure," I replied.

"Jim, you think there's Spanish treasure down there?" Kenny asked.

"Kenny, how in the hell am I supposed to know that? Maybe this is where Gasparilla's ship went down!"

"Oh, come on, Jim! You don't expect me to fall for that old tale, do you?"

"Well, I would think there's as much chance of that as there is of there being any Spanish treasure out here. From what I've seen on TV those Spanish treasure fleets usually wrecked when they got blown by a storm onto a reef- not, when they were sailing along in over a hundred feet of water."

"Okay, guys," Doc asked, "so if it's not for Indian artifacts, and if it's not for Spanish treasure, why is Jocko diving out here? Why is he diving in this exact spot?"

"I've got no clue," I answered. "What's the bottom look like?"

"It looks flat on the sonar. I see one thing moving on the fish finder- but, that's probably just Jocko swimming around. It doesn't look like that good of a spot to fish to me."

"Then why are we still here?" Kenny said, with a hint of fisherman's frustration starting to show.

"Do you think we should stick around to see if Jocko needs any help?" I asked.

"No, I don't think so," Doc replied. "Kenny says that he goes diving all the time and I don't see anything that appears to be out of the ordinary. And, besides, if he really is looking for treasure out here he probably wouldn't be all at that happy to see us on his spot when he surfaced. He might think that we're trying to muscle in on his mother lode."

"So, you think we should just go on our way?" I asked.

"I would recommend that we move on to fish some other spots that are further to the south. We can come back by here on our way home. If there's still no sign of him then we can alert the Coast Guard, or something. If he's gone, then we'll know all was well. And, if he's sitting on his boat drinking beer we'll just pretend that we happened by. Agreed?"

"Let's go fishing!" Kenny answered.

"Jim?"

"I'm okay with that."

Chapter Thirteen

Twenty five minutes later we were drifting over a spot identified on the chart plotter as "Jose's Favorite.' Thirty minutes later it was one of ours as well. We had each put at least one very large grouper in the box, and had hooked up with, and lost, a number of other sizeable fish. We were all breathing hard, sweating, and ready for a break when Doc suggested that we should move to repeat the drift. We all readily agreed. Kenny stepped to the cooler, in which we had iced down beer and water, and asked what we wanted.

"Water for me, Kenny," I replied.

Doc said that he'd take a beer, to which Kenny quickly replied that he'd have one, too- since he always hated to see a man drinking alone. Doc steered the boat slowly to where our drift had begun, taking a little time more than strictly necessary, just so we could all cool down and recover.

As we slowly motored I asked, "Doc, what was the name of that spot where Jocko's boat was anchored?"

"I think it was 'B-26,' Doc replied. "Why?"

"That's what I thought. Now, I'm just wondering, and I know that this is a long shot, but after our lunch with Ernie I started doing, like I told you I would, some research about Cuba. You know, I just wanted to re-familiarize myself about how Castro came to power, and all that kind of stuff. Anyway, as I was doing that, I learned some interesting stuff."

"Like what?"

"Well, have you ever heard the story about 'Batista's Lost Gold Flight'?"

Doc quickly looked in my direction. I could tell that I now had his undivided attention.

"Fulgencio Batista, as I'm sure you know, was the President of Cuba before he was overthrown by Fidel Castro's rebels. He, of course, was a dictator. But, he was generally supported by the US government, and he also had a very close relationship with Santo Trafficante and the American Mafia. On December 31, 1958, as the rebels closed in on Havana, Batista threw a New Year's Eve party for his cabinet and other top officials. Then, at midnight, he surprised those in attendance by announcing that he was officially renouncing his presidency, and that he would be leaving the country that night. Shortly after, at three that morning, Batista, and 40 of his family and supporters, boarded a Cuban passenger plane, and flew to the Dominican Republic. Another plane flew out shortly afterwards filled with government ministers, Army officers, and the Governor of Havana. That much is commonly known. But, what is not as widely known is that a flight of four Cuban military B-26s secretly left Havana that night- in route for MacDill Air Force base in Tampa, Florida. Rumors have it that these planes were loaded with gold, gems, and artwork- essentially, the whole wealth of the Cuban Treasury. The plan was for the CIA to take possession of this fortune, to safeguard it, and to keep it out of the hands of the rebels. Three of these planes supposedly made it to Tampa safely that night. But, the fourth was never seen again. Some believe that it crashed in the Gulf of Mexico; some believe it went down in the Everglades; and some even contend that it was diverted, either by the mob or by elements within the CIA, to a secret landing field in South Florida. Rumor has it that many millions of dollars went missing that night. That lost fortune has never been found."

"Oh, come on, Jim! You're not trying to tell me that Jocko is over there diving for that treasure right now, are you?"

"Doc, clearly I don't know, but that spot was labeled 'B-26' on your chart, either by an old Cuban named Ernie, or by some other old Cuban who gave the chart to him. And, if you look at the chart, and then draw a straight line between Havana and MacDill, it will pretty much pass right over that spot on the chart. All this could, of course, be a mere coincidence. And, Jocko could indeed only be looking for Gasparilla's flagship! I would say that is certainly possible. But, I'd think, it would just not be very likely."

Kenny, who had been listening quietly to all of this, now asked, "But, how would Jocko ever know to dive in that exact spot?"

"Kenny, I guess that I forgot to tell you, but the night Irma came through someone broke into my house and stole the chart that Ernie gave me."

"What? You think Jocko stole your chart?"

"I don't know. But, someone stole it, for sure. And now, Jocko's anchored exactly over a spot marked on that chart."

"Why that conniving little bastard!"Kenny exclaimed. "Why don't we just go over there, and beat his ass?"

"Kenny, we can't do that. Besides, he's already got the number, and he's probably already thrown the chart away. There's no way we could ever prove anything. He'd just have us arrested. Back in the old days, back when there were pirates in these waters, that's probably exactly what we'd have done. But, you just can't do that kind of stuff anymore. Besides, were all around seventy years old, and to various degrees, we're approaching becoming decrepit. Jocko, on the other hand, looks like a pretty fit, hard working, lean and mean, forty year-old. Things might not exactly go in our favor."

"So what *are* we going to do?" Kenny asked.

"We're simply going to start another drift and catch our limit of grouper. Then, we'll go back by Jocko's boat- you know, just to check to make sure he's okay. Then, depending on how that goes, we're going to go back home and think about what to do next?"

By the time we'd caught our limit, and gone back to 'B-26,' Jocko's boat was already gone. Why had he left? Did that mean that there was nothing on the bottom? Or, had he headed back in to organize how to swiftly and secretly bring the treasure to the surface? As we'd slowly circled the marked location, intently studying an unrevealing sonar screen, I think all of us really wanted to jump in and swim to the bottom- just to see for ourselves what was down there. But, none of us actually knew how to dive- and, of course, even if we'd been willing to fake it we didn't have any diving equipment with us.

"Doc," I asked, "What if we rented some tanks? Do you think you could get to the bottom?"

"Maybe. But, if I did, I'm pretty sure that I'd never get back up- I'm claustrophobic as hell. There's no way that I'm diving that deep."

"We could tie a line around your ankle," Kenny suggested helpfully.

"Nope. I'm not doing it," Doc said with a tinge of severe finality. "How about you, Kenny? You seem like you might still be crazy enough to do something like this."

"In my younger days, sure. But, not now. You may not remember, but I've only got one lung left. I have enough trouble breathing on dry land- much less a hundred feet down. But, Jim, how about you? Apart from being a little portly you seem like you're in pretty good health. If we strapped a bunch of lead on you would you take a little dive for the group?"

"Kenny, I'd love to. In fact, I've actually tried to get certified on a couple of occasions. I passed all the tests, and excelled in the pool. But, as soon as I attempted to do a "deep water check out dive" my right ear drum collapsed. Caused so much vertigo I was lucky to make it back to the surface. There's no way that I could do it."

"So, where does that leave us?" Kenny asked.

"I don't know," Doc replied. "Let's just go in and think about it."

Chapter Fourteen

That evening, before dinner, I called Mike Collins. Doc, Kenny and I had agreed that we needed to let the Sherriff's Office know what we suspected. I'd lost the vote about who should make the call.

But, the rings went unanswered. I left a voicemail that simply asked him to call me, at his convenience. Somewhat relieved that I wouldn't have to immediately suffer through another dose of his semi-friendly insults and jibes, I put the phone down, and walked into the kitchen to fix myself the first of my nightly "scotch and waters," prepared in my customary tall insulated Tervis tumbler. As I poured the comforting amber fluid over the crackling cubes I reflected on how my taste in Scotch whisky had evolved since retirement. Actually, I had to admit, it wasn't so much that my tastes had changed- it was more about how having to live on a pension no longer allowed me to afford the delicious and unique top-shelf single malts that I'd always loved. In fact, as the realities of retirement had become more and more apparent, I'd even moved down the shelves at 'Doc Watson's' (our popular and friendly island liquor store, more commonly known as The Doctor's Office) in terms of what blended whisky I poured. Whereas before I'd always been a fan of "Johnny Walker's" smokier blends, now I seemed to be more frequently drinking the slightly less expensive (and slightly less tasty) "Famous Grouse," or "Grant's." I hadn't sunk to buying off the bottom shelf yet, I mused, but with the clear understanding that I was probably only a few years away from being forced to make that move.

As I filled my glass I took care to stay out of Jill's way as she moved rapidly around our small kitchen. She was happily, and purposefully, focused on arranging and preparing what I knew would be a delicious dinner. As I contemplated what was taking place- me pouring myself a whisky, Jill preparing dinner- I hoped that I wasn't really as much of a chauvinist as current activities suggested that I might be. Regardless, I knew that I was an extremely fortunate man. I was happily married- to a beautiful woman- who was also a great cook! Maybe, I thought, I *was* a chauvinist- a very lucky chauvinist!

"Jill," I asked, "do you think that I am a chauvinist?"

She turned to look at me, with a slightly surprised, and amused, look on her face. Then she slowly raised her right eyebrow in a way that warned me that I might not be especially pleased with her upcoming reply- a response that I knew would be intelligent, and would likely cut right to the bone with its uncompromised insight. I braced myself. She had just opened her mouth to respond when the phone rang.

"Hold that thought, dear," I interrupted. "That's probably Mike Collins returning my call." A quick glance at my caller ID confirmed that assumption.

"Hey, Mike," I said as I clicked on. "Thanks for getting back. Hope I didn't interrupt anything."

"Not a problem, Jim. I've been anticipating your call."

"You have?"

"I assumed that you, and the "Mango Dumpling Gang," would eventually find another body, sooner or later. So, who is it this time?

"Sorry to disappoint, Mike, but we've got no body. But, I think we have something that might be even better!"

"Wait! Let me guess. Does this have to do with that old fishing chart someone took from your buddy's garage?"

"As a matter of fact, it does!" I gladly replied, happy that Mike had steered the conversation in this direction without first subjecting me to another round of ridicule. "Actually, we think we may know who stole it, and why?"

"Jeez! I know better than to ask- I really do. But, which powerful politician, or popular pillar of the community do you suspect this time? Isn't that the way that these things always start with you?"

"No, no- wait, Mike. This time it's nothing like that. This time it's just a normal guy who lives here in St. James City. I swear."

"Jim, you can stop right there. I already know that you're lying."

"Mike, I'm not lying to you. That hurts me. Why would you say that?"

"It's simple. You see, after years of working this area as a detective, I know for a fact that there are not any *normal* people that live in St. James City."

"Mike, stop laughing. And, please, just quit trying to be so damn cute. It's really unbecoming for a man in your line of work."

"Come on, Jim. You don't really think that a crusty old cop like me would ever try to be cute, do you? And, I can assure you that there is no way that I would ever be worried about being perceived as 'unbecoming.' Hell, I don't even know what that word means. But, the last thing I would ever want is for you, my trusted confidant, (in my mind I could see the laughing sparkle in his rolling eyes as he'd made this last statement) to feel that he can't confide in me to assist the Lee County Sherriff's Department in its pursuit of justice. So- just tell me, Jim, which of St. James City's many distinguished residents do you think may have purloined Doc's missing map?"

For a moment I contemplated whether I wanted to continue the bantering contest, but decided, since I'd likely eventually lose it anyway, not to do that.

"Actually, we think that a fellow in town, a sailor and diver by the name of Jocko Smith, probably took it."

"Jocko!" Mike exclaimed.

"You know Jocko?" I asked.

"Oh, hell yeah! Everybody, of course, knows Jocko. He's been around town a long time. In fact, in my opinion he's one of the nicest guys you'll ever meet- you can tell that by the way that he treats his dog. He blew in on his big sail boat one day, and I guess he just likes it here. He has never left. Now, he and his dog spend their days working down at the boat yard, and their nights anchoring one end of "The Short Bus" bar at Woody's. What's his dog's name?"

"I believe its 'Bingo'" I replied.

"Yeah, that's it!" Mike responded. "And, what's the name of his boat?"

"The Lady Chatterley," I answered.

"Yep. I've always thought that was a cool name for a boat. You know he likes telling the ladies that he meets at the bar that he's "Lady Chatterley's Lover"! I don't really know what that means, but, from what I've observed, it seems to be a pretty effective pick up line. Do you know what it means, Jim?"

"I think it's kind of a literary reference, Mike. Not that surprised that you wouldn't be familiar with it (now, my eyes were sparkling). My guess would be that it probably works better with the intellectual- type ladies."

"No, not necessarily (now I could hear him softly chuckling) - at least not based on what I've observed," answered Mike. "But, what makes you think that Jocko stole the chart?"

"Well, it's simple. When we were out in the Gulf today, Jocko's boat was anchored squarely on top of one of the spots marked on that chart."

"Come on, Jim. You can do better than that. You know as well as I do that those good grouper numbers get shared around. The fact that he was anchored on one of the spots you wanted to fish hardly gives me, or you, a credible reason to suspect someone of theft. You'll have to come up with something better than that?"

"But, Mike, hear me out. This wasn't just some ordinary grouper number! We think that...." By this time I could tell that I was beginning to become a little excited, and slightly exasperated- never a good thing when you're talking with an experienced cop. But, I couldn't help myself. I was so anxious to tell Mike about what we suspected was the real reason behind the theft.

"Hold on, Mike, let take a breath, and just slow down for a minute. This is important. You need to listen carefully to what I'm going to tell you."

"Okay, "Jim. I'm all ears. But, please, no more bodies!"

I could hear him laughing to himself again as he said that. I took a sip of whisky to settle my nerves.

"Alright," I began. "No bodies.... oh, well, ... I guess that I can't really make that promise. You know, there might just actually be some bodies involved in this before it's all said and done. But, honestly, I have no bodies to report at this time."

"Honestly? Does that mean you've been dishonest the rest of the time? Jim, what the hell are you talking about? Just how many scotches have you already had tonight?"

"Mike- I haven't even had one yet. Truthfully..... Oh hell..... look Mike, I'm just starting on my first.....so please ..... Just shut up, and listen. We are convinced that this is all tied to a hunt for missing treasure!"

The line went silent. I guessed that whatever Mike Collins had been expecting to hear from me it wasn't this. Or, maybe, more likely, he was trying to figure out how to be able to exit, before it was too late, what he knew was going to become another confusing, embarrassing, and possibly career-threatening investigation.

Finally, he responded. "Jim, I must not have heard you correctly. You didn't say missing treasure, did you?"

"Yeah, Mike. Actually, that is exactly what I said. We think that the chart showed where there may be a fortune in the Gulf in lost gold."

"So- let me guess- you and your nearly senile buddies think ya'll have now stumbled across where 'The Floriblanca,' Jose Gaspar's flagship, sank? Am I right?"

"No, Mike- that is not why I called. Just knockoff the nonsense- this is serious stuff. We may have found the location of Batista's lost gold?"

The line went quiet- again. Then, before he finally spoke, I could hear what sounded like a deep exasperated sigh.

"Jim, you do know don't you, that this is not the first time that this lost fortune has been discovered?"

"Shit! You mean that all the gold has already been recovered?"

"Well- not exactly. Jim, having only been down here for a few years you probably don't know this, but this story is one of those Florida myths that just won't die. Every ten years or so, someone new, usually someone credible, claims to have finally located that damn plane that may, or may not actually be missing. Then, the news media gets hold of the story, and they work everyone up. Before long everybody's got 'gold fever!' Eventually, it's always been shown to be a mistake, or a farce- there's never, ever, been any gold. So, I hate to be the bearer of bad news, but you guys probably shouldn't count on getting rich quick as a result of your amazing discovery."

"But, we think the location of the plane is shown on the chart that was stolen."

"You bring up any pieces of the plane yet?"

"No. None of us dive. But, we think that's why Jocko was out there. He may have brought something up."

"Jim, let me share with you what happened the last times someone 'found' this plane. It was a little over ten years ago. A local commercial fisherman had been looking for this plane for almost thirty years. Back in 1990, he marked a spot on his chart that looked like it had structure. You know it was just a spot that looked like it could have fish on it. In fact, it did, and he fished there all summer. But, then he hooked and brought up a piece of what looked like it might have come from an airplane- a military plane. So, of course, he decided to dive on the site. What he found on the bottom were two machine gun turrets, two engines, and a B-26 wing. But, the plane's fuselage was missing. He dove on that location for years, looking for gold- but, he never found a damn thing. Then, a hurricane came through, and it shifted so much sand on the bottom that all evidence of the plane totally disappeared. At that point there was nothing more that the fisherman could do by himself. He still believed that the gold was probably down there, but he didn't have the resources to look any further. Eventually, he got to talking to a guy in a bar down in Naples. Jim, you know, of course, that all great treasure hunting stories eventually involve guys talking in a bar? I'm kind of surprised that you haven't mentioned that yet in your story. But, anyway, as it turns out this guy was from Chicago- he was retired, rich, bored, and very intrigued by the idea of finding lost treasure. This wasn't long after Mel Fisher had found the wreck of the 'Atocha.' So, before long these guys and some of their friends had formed a corporation, invested in the equipment they'd need to move underwater sand, and gone treasure hunting. Eventually, they were able to find most of the plane, even though debris from the crash was scattered over a quarter mile area of sea floor. They were even able to determine, through flight forensic analysis, that one of the plane's propellers had probably malfunctioned, and that this was likely the cause of the high speed crash. Jim, do you want to know how all this turned out?"

"Of course, but since you told me earlier that no one's ever found any gold- I'm guessing that they didn't either."

"Very good, Jim. That shows that you're paying attention. But, you know what they did find? Eventually, they found a plaque on the plane that had the craft's serial number on it. When they researched that they found that this was not a Cuban plan at all. Rather the plaque was attached to a US Army plane that had crashed on a routine training mission in 1942. The plane had taken off from Fort Myers Army Air Base, from what is now known as Page Field, with a crew of six. A little less than an hour after it had taken off the base received a radio call that the crew was bailing out. This was a brand new plane; with a well-trained, if inexperienced, pilot; and the weather was good. Eventually, search teams found the bodies of the pilot and the co-pilot, but there was no sign of the remainder of the crew, or of the plane. And, there was never an explanation for why the plane had crashed."

"That's interesting, Mike. But, why are you telling me all this?"

"I guess, because, I don't want any of us to get too excited about ya'll finding Batista's Gold. You do know, don't you, that there's no real evidence that this treasure flight ever happened? Or, even if it did, that one of the planes actually crashed in the Gulf?"

"Yeah. But, what about the damn chart? What about the spot marked on it? It's located directly on a straight line between Havana and Tampa, and its clearly labeled, undoubtedly by an old Cuban, 'B-26'! I would think that for would be enough for the Sherriff's Department to want to investigate this. I would think that ya'll would want to send out a dive team to see what's down there."

"And, Jim, your thinking, as usual, would be wrong. There's no way that the Sherriff would want to see his office publicly tied to a 'wild goose chase' treasure hunt way out in the Gulf of Mexico. Can you imagine what the 'News Press' would do with that? Or, what his political opponents would do with that at election time? I don't think we could even pass something like that off as just a training exercise. So- there's nothing I can do for you to help you see what's on the bottom. But, I do appreciate you letting me know about Jocko. I have to admit that the pieces do seem to maybe point in his direction. So, I'll keep all this in mind, and if anything comes of it, I'll keep you posted."

"Fair enough, Mike. That's really all I wanted. And, thanks for the history lesson."

"My pleasure, Jim. Please pass along my regards to Jill."

"Will do. Have a good night."

"Jim, I couldn't help but listen in to your conversation with Mike," Jill said. "So, do you really think that Jocko stole Doc's chart so he could hunt for gold?"

"It's just a theory," I replied. "But, unless it was just a coincidence, I don't know why else he would be anchored and diving on that exact spot."

"Jim, tell me again about that spot, and why you think there could be gold on it."

I filled her in on my understanding about the events that had led up to this.

"So," Jill asked, "exactly how much gold do you think could be there on the bottom?"

"That's a good question. Out on the boat we were hoping for billions. But, that was probably just the beer talking. I don't even know if that would be possible. Let's do the math."

I picked up my I-pad, and Googled "payload capacity B-26." A second later I found that the plane had been designed to carry up to 5,500 pounds of bombs, although in practice it rarely carried this heavy of a load on a mission since doing so compromised both the plane's range and maneuverability. Next, I researched how the weight of gold was measured, quickly learning that the standard for weighing precious metals was a 'troy' ounce. I was surprised to learn that this was a slightly heavier measure than the standard one that we use for weighing sugar, or grain, ... or bombs. In fact, there are only about 14.6 troy ounces in a standard pound. I used the calculator feature to convert the plane's cargo capacity into troy ounces- eighty thousand, three hundred. Next, I found that the current price for an ounce of gold was $1,250. Multiplying these factors generated a number that was slightly north of one hundred million dollars.

"That's not a billion," Jill observed.

"No, it's not. But, still- that's a heck of a lot of money."

"Yeah. So, what are ya'll going to do now?"

"Jill, I have no idea. I'll talk with the guys tomorrow, and see what we come up with."

"Well, maybe I'll just do down to Woody's tomorrow night. You know, I can go down to place a to-go order for dinner, and sit at the side bar to have a drink while I wait."

"Why would you want to do that?"

"Jim, you know as well as I do that all the cool locals sit at the "Short Bus. As a matter of fact, Jocko's usually there most nights."

"You know Jocko?"

"Of course! I know all the 'cool' guys!"

"Oh, you do, do you? And, you think Jocko's cool?"

"Well, just, kind of. But, of course, he's not nearly as cool as you, Jim. (I appreciated her attempt, even if it was transparent and obvious, to ease the bruise of my ego.) But, I really do think that his dog, Bingo, is super cool! I love the way that he lays quietly under the neighboring table whenever Jocko sits at the bar. So, I always try to talk to him, and rub his head, when I see Jocko at the bar."

"You rub Jocko's head?!!!!"

"Not Jocko, you dummy!" Jill exclaimed. "I always rub Bingo's head. Now, let's have some dinner. It's getting cold."

Chapter Fifteen

"Good morning, Doc!" I had called at eight, trying to be civilized, yet anxious to update him on my conversation with Lt. Collins.

"And, a good morning it is, Jim. To what do I owe the honor of hearing your cheerful voice?"

"Wow! Given your pleasant greeting I'd say that you and Miss Peg must have had a great night."

"Jim, every night with Miss Peg is a great night. What's up?"

"Just wanted to let you know that I talked with Mike Collins last night. Told him about Jocko being anchored on top of 'B-26.'"

"And?"

"He didn't seem to be all that impressed with either that coincidence, or with the story about Batista's Gold. He actually cautioned me to not spend any of it yet."

"But, what about Jocko? Is he going to do anything about it?"

"Nope. But, he said that he'd keep it in mind."

"Well, Jim, I guess that's better than nothing. You got any better ideas this morning?"

"Actually, I may. Jill offered to go to Woody's tonight and try to spend some time with Jocko over on the 'Short Bus.' But, it occurred to me right before I woke up this morning that maybe she ought to invite Jocko over to the house for dinner. You and Peggy, Kenny and Janice would, of course, be invited, too. What do you think?"

"I think that would be a great idea. We should at least be able to figure out if he's lying."

"Okay. I'll have her make it happen. Now, what about the lunch with Ernie? Do you have any snapper?"

Of course, I do. But, it's all frozen. I was thinking we ought to try to catch some fresh snapper for Ernie. What do you think?"

"Fresh is always better- no question there. And, I'll be glad to help. When are you thinking about going?"

"I want to check with Kenny to see what his schedule is. But, we're going to have lunch on Wednesday, so I was thinking about going out Tuesday afternoon. There's going to be a good outgoing tide then. How's that work for you?"

"Hey, as long as I don't have a doctor's appointment, I'm always good. My calendar's clear. Are you planning to go offshore?"

"No, I don't think so. It looks like the winds are going to be blowing a little. Nothing too bad, but just enough to make it uncomfortable in the Gulf. A friend recently told me about a spot up on the north end of the island. I've been wanting to try it. He said it's loaded with big Mangrove Snapper- sometimes some other stuff, too."

"Sounds like a plan. Just text me when you get everything arranged with Kenny."

Two days later Kenny and I were heading north in Doc's twenty one foot bay boat. It was a sweet ride with a brand new, super quiet, two hundred horsepower Suzuki providing more than adequate propulsion. Doc had spared no expense in equipping the boat. It had an aluminum jack plate that could effortlessly raise the engine six inches whenever required to negotiate the sound's shallows. It had a Power Pole shallow water anchoring system, and a slick, eight foot long, electric trolling motor. He had also equipped the boat with an over the top, eleven inch wide, Garmin GPS Sonar system. No question that this was a very nice rig for fishing Pine Island Sound.

Our only concerns, as we pointed the bow towards 'the power lines,' were avoiding a squall line which at that exact moment was drenching Bokeelia and where to find schools of 'white bait.' Initially, our plan had been to net the bait on the shoals that line the northern end of the Sound, but the threatening rain had caused us to reevaluate that decision. Therefore, we elected to pull into the shallows that line the bay's western edge- between Red Fish and Captiva passes. At the least it would help to pass some time as the rain drifted to the north, and, possibly also allow us to fill our bait wells.

I volunteered to throw the cast net; Kenny offered to chum. Doc would help with sorting the bait once it was on board. The net was ten foot long, with quarter inch mesh- perfect for white bait. I had to smile to myself thinking about the one time I threw a three-eighths inch mesh net on top of a huge school of bait. A great many of those fish gilled themselves in the net as they struggled to escape. The only way to then get them out of the net was basically to pull their heads off. It was a mess, and a waste of a lot of innocent bait lives. Moral of that story- never use anything other than a quarter inch mesh bait net.

While I was getting organized with the net, Kenny had mixed a bucketful of dried fish meal with a little sea water, creating a dough that he could form into balls of chum. He was already methodically throwing them towards the spot where I would want to throw the net once he'd enticed the bait to appear. It didn't take long. Three or four minutes later we could begin to see fleeting silver flashes in the tannin stained water. Another minute later there were enough flashes for me to justifying throwing the net. While I'd thrown a net my entire life I was using today a new technique that my friend Terry had recently taught me. I placed the lead line from the bottom of the net under my left armpit, while holding some of the net and lead line in my right hand, just as I had always done. I had been very impressed watching Terry throw his net in this fashion, and I was anxious to give it a try. This technique forces you to keep your left elbow close to your body, which in turn allows the net to spread more fully when you rotate to make your cast. As the net left my hands I was delighted that the technique worked as promised. I had thrown a beautiful, perfectly round, full net spread, and it was positioned exactly where we'd last seen silver flashes.

I let the net settle to the bottom before beginning to slowly and smoothly pull in the hand line. The top of the net had hardly broken the surface before it was obvious that we now had all the bait we would need to fish that day. There looked to be several hundred white baits in the net. In addition, there were also an assortment of other types of small fry that would need to be picked out and thrown back in- green backs, trumpet fish, and a dozen or so small pin fish. We wouldn't need any of those today. Ten minutes later the white bait were busily swimming in their new, now constantly aerating, bait well home. While Doc and Kenny tended to the bait, I used a bucket to dip seawater and flushed the deck clean of the seaweed and other detritus that had come onboard in the net. When we finally finished our respective tasks and looked up we could see that the storm had drifted northward into Charlotte Harbor. It was time to go fishing.

"All right, Doc," I said. "Where's this new snapper hole you've been telling us about?"

"Jim, it's on the north end of the island. You want to see it on the chart?"

"Yeah. So, you've already got it loaded on the chart?"

"I loaded the lats and longs as soon as my friend told me about it. I labeled it 'Mullet Boat.' Here take a look?"

I could see the labeled spot on the chart. It seemed to be in middle of a narrow, but deep, channel that wound through the shallows towards the Harbor.

"Doc, I thought we were going to catch snapper. Why are we going to a mullet hole?"

"You'll see. Now, hold on tight. This new Suzuki wants to run."

A few minutes later we were on the north end of the island, anchored front and rear, about thirty feet up-tide of the spot on the chart. The port side of the boat was presented to the spot that we wanted to fish. Kenny was on the bow, I was on the stern. Doc was positioned in the middle, ready to offer assistance providing fresh bait, unhooking catfish, putting snapper in the live well, or even bringing out the landing net should that type of assistance be required.

"Okay, Guys," Doc said, "put a piece of white bait on, and cast out about thirty feet or so. Let it go to the bottom and let the tide carry it on top of the boat that's sunk out there. According to what I've been told you should have bite almost immediately."

Kenny and I did as we were instructed. We were both fishing with small wire circle hooks- not big enough for anything really large, but extremely sharp and almost guaranteed to imbed themselves securely in the lips and jaws of any snapper foolish enough to eat our bait.

As we waited for the small flashing fish to settle towards the bottom I asked Doc, "What do you mean that there's a boat sunk out there? What kind of boat is it?"

"My friend told me that it was an overloaded mullet boat. It sank as it was heading back to Bokeelia- loaded to the gunwales with gillnetted fish."

"This happen recently, Doc?"

"No. It sank back before the net ban went into effect. I guess that by now most people have forgotten that it's even out here."

The history lesson was interrupted by Kenny yelling excitedly- "Whoa, whoa. That's a nice fish."

His medium light weight rod was bent into a semi-circle by the pull. Shortly thereafter a beautiful fourteen inch snapper was in the boat. In the meantime I also had a strong bite, but the fish had managed to avoid the hook and had escaped with the bait. This type of action continued unabated for the next hour by which time we'd caught our limit. We had more than enough fresh snapper filets for the lunch tomorrow with Ernie.

Having both time and bait left we decided to move south down the Sound to fish for trout. I suggested to Doc that he steer towards the deep water grass flats in front of the old fish shacks. I knew that there were usually big speckled trout in that area- hiding along the channel edges, anxious to ambush any careless white baits that intruded in their territory. My hunch was right- soon we had a box full of both trout. It was time to head home and clean fish.

Chapter Sixteen

The next morning, slightly before noon, Doc and I once again drove north to Ernie's house. In the back seat was a cooler in which we'd iced the bag of snapper filets and two six packs of Hatuey beer. We were very much looking forward to enjoying the delicious recipe that Ernie had promised.

As we parked in the rock drive we could see our Cuban friend standing in the shade of the trees and tending the fire in his grill. I could see that already there were a couple of pots, and large skillets, heating on the grate. Again, a clean white towel was draped over Ernie's shoulder. When he heard us arrive, he wiped his hands, placed the towel on the table, and walked towards us- a smile on his face.

We quickly shook hands, and exchanged polite hugs of welcome.

Ernie spoke first, "Thank you so much for coming. I have been looking forward to this all week."

"So have we," Doc and I enthused together in reply.

"Ernie," Doc said, "we have brought the snapper filets, just as you requested. They are fresh, never frozen- we caught them for you yesterday."

"Doc, I knew from watching and listening to you that you were a fisherman. I never had any doubts that you would bring fish. I assume from the way that the wind was blowing yesterday that you caught them in the Sound."

"Yes. Just a little north of Patricio Island. I know a hole there that has an old sunken boat in it. It was loaded with fish."

"This wouldn't be the 'Mullet Boat' hole would it?"

Doc's eyes opened in amazement. "You mean that you know about that spot?"

"I used to fish it many years ago. In fact, I knew the men who sunk the boat there. It was a pretty rotten boat anyway so they just left it. There was no motor on it- they'd been towing it behind their big boat. But, that's neither here nor there- I'm just glad you were able to catch some fresh fish. How was the water? Any sign of red tide?"

"Not where we were. But, from what I understand it's still pretty bad outside of Boca Grande Pass."

"That's a shame. Jim, that's a large cooler you're carrying for just a few pounds of fish filets."

"Actually, Ernie, we also brought you a couple of six packs of Hatuey- just in case you were hot and thirsty."

Ernie laughed. "You really are gentlemen, and, as a matter of fact, I am very thirsty!"

"Excellent," I replied. "Let's put the cooler down in the shade and then I'll see what I can do to take care of that problem."

A minute later we each had an icy beer in hand. Ernie had returned to tending the grill, carefully stirring whatever was cooking in the pots and skillet. Doc and I had taken a seat at the table.

"Ernie," Doc said. "You promised us that you'd prepare a delicious recipe for the snapper. From what I smell you are well on your way to keeping that promise. What are you making?"

"Doc, this is just a simple Cuban fisherman's dish. It's called 'Hachinango Enlchilado'- or, in English, Cuban-style snapper filets. Onions, tomatoes, peppers, olives, garlic, and a few other ingredients stewed together. When that cooks down a bit I'll add the filets. Then, when it's done we'll serve it over white rice, along with a side of fried ripe plantains. Cuban food doesn't get much more traditional than this."

"Ernie," I said. "That sounds wonderful. Can I give you a hand with anything?"

"No, Jim. You just relax and enjoy your beer. It won't be too long now."

"Ernie," Doc began, "If you don't mind we've had some developments concerning the stolen chart. I know you told me that you didn't want to talk about it anymore, but I thought you'd like to know what has happened."

Ernie looked Doc in the eyes before nodding slowly to silently convey that he should continue.

Doc then began to explain how we had found Jocko anchored over the spot on the chart marked as 'B-26.'

I was carefully watching Ernie's eyes all the while that Doc was telling him what had happened. I was sure that in them I could sense an intense interest in what Doc was saying. Then I thought I glimpsed what might have been a fleeting grimace cross Ernie's face. This was followed by an almost imperceptible slow side to side shake of his head.

When Doc finished, Ernie spoke. "Gentlemen, I feel that I must apologize for having put you in this distress. I can see now that it was my fault. As you know, I am now becoming old, and, unfortunately, increasingly ill. I guess that those two things are causing me to not be as alert, and as careful, as I always have been. Let me tell you what I think must have happened. You see, I know Jocko Smith. Not well. But, for some reason, we frequently seem to end up at the barber shop on the same day at the same time. I guess we must have standing appointments that put us there together every month. A few months back, a little before Irma came through, I remember having my hair cut, while Jocko was sitting in a chair waiting his turn. I was talking, as I always do, with Luis, the barber. I was talking too much, but he and I go way back- he is Cuban, too. He was too young to have served in the Brigade, but his older brother did. His brother Julio was in a different Battalion, but still I knew him from training in

Guatemala. His brother didn't survive- he was killed in the swamp after the fighting was over. He was murdered, really- but, that's neither here nor there. Luis and I, whenever I get my hair cut, like to talk about the old days. And, of course, we talk in Spanish- I guess it just makes us feel young again. And, as we Cuban's sometimes do, we do tend to become a little excited, and sometimes a little argumentative. That day I remember that we were arguing, for some unknown reason, about whether Batista's treasure flight really took place. Luis was adamant that it had never happened- he was convinced that Batista had already looted the treasury before he left for the Dominican Republic. I was even more adamant that the flight had actually taken place. Finally, I guess just to show off a little, and against my better judgment that this was a subject that I should not talk about, I told Luis that I knew for a fact that the flight had happened because my cousin Carlos had been a co-pilot in one of the planes. Then, and I can't really believe now that I was that stupid, I bragged to Luis that I even knew where the lost plane had crashed because my cousin had given me the coordinates of exactly where he thought he'd seen the plane go down. I told him that I had plotted that location on a fishing chart that I'd been given. All of this was said in Spanish, of course. I guess that I must have assumed that Jocko wouldn't have any idea of what we were talking about. Finally, Luis told me I was just a crazy old man that was starting to go soft in the head. That led us down another argumentative path that we explored until Luis had finished with my hair. Now, I just really can't believe I was that foolish. But, at least you and your wife weren't hurt. I'm thankful for that."

"Ernie," Doc exclaimed, "you mean to tell me that there really was a gold flight, and that the spot you marked on the chart is where the lost plane went down? That's important information!"

"The spot I marked is only where my cousin guessed that the plane might have gone down. He had no instruments then to know exactly where they were. He admits himself that the spot he gave me could have been off from the actual crash site by twenty, or more, miles- in any direction. That's a lot of ocean."

"That is a lot of ocean!" Doc replied. "But, at least we know that the lost gold is out there somewhere."

"Well," Ernie responded, "all we really know is that something is out there. My cousin never actually knew what had been loaded onto any of the planes."

"But, still," I said, "I'm guessing that he knew something was on the planes, and that it was heavy. So, it is possible that it might be!"

"Yes, Jim," Ernie agreed. "It might be."

"So, Ernie" I continued, "You think that Jocko overheard this conversation and then stole the chart?"

"It's possible, I suppose," Ernie said. "But, I don't even know if he speaks Spanish. For all I know Luis could have told the story to his next customer."

"But," Doc interrupted, "what I don't understand is how Jocko would know that you had given that chart to me?"

"I'm afraid that that is my fault, also," Ernie said, with another grimace and a sheepish look now on his face. "I remember trying to downplay the significance of this information by telling Luis that I was thinking about just giving it to you. Luis had quite a laugh about that, saying that that just proved that what'd I'd been saying was a fabrication. I laughed then, too. I made a point to not disagree with Luis' assessment."

"We can find out easily enough if Jocko speaks Spanish," I said. "Jill is going to invite him over to our house for dinner. Doc and his wife Peg are going to be there, too. She speaks Spanish fluently. It shouldn't take her long to find out if Jocko does, too. But, enough about the damn lost chart. How is the snapper coming? I don't want it to be overcooked."

"Get your plates, gentlemen. Everything is ready."

Chapter Seventeen

As we finished Ernie's delicious meal I finally brought up the subject that I'd been waiting to discuss.

"Ernie, the last time we were here you mentioned having trained on Useppa in preparation for joining the brigade that assaulted Cuba at the Bay of Pigs. If you feel up to discussing that further I know that Doc and I would love to learn more about that experience."

"Yes, Jim, I remember my promise to tell you more about that, and I've actually been looking forward to sharing with you what I can remember from that time. I don't get to do that much anymore. Last week I told you about how we came to the island in early June, 1960- blindfolded, in the dead of night. At that time we had no idea where we were. Eventually, there were sixty six of us Cubans on the island- at one time, or another. There was maybe a third that many Americans- a few Special Forces soldiers, some CIA officers, some guards, and at least a dozen doctors and psychologists.

We woke up so excited our first morning on the island. We'd slept in a deserted, dilapidated old building beside what had once been the golf course. But, that didn't matter- my friend Juan and I were just thankful that we'd been brought to the island to train to fight against Castro. But, as we met the other Cubans, and talked with the Americans, we quickly learned that was not exactly what we were there for- at least not yet. We would eventually get that type of training, but that would come later.

For the next three weeks we were repeatedly evaluated, and tested. We took dozens of lie detector tests; we took aptitude tests; we took what we guessed were intelligence tests; and we were subjected, again and again, to numerous types of physical exams and challenges. From all of this, we deduced that whoever was in charge was trying to determine if we could be trusted, and if so, what roles should we play in the plan. Some of the Cubans that were there had clearly already been identified to serve as the highest level officers and leaders of the effort to overthrow Castro. For example, Manuel Artime was there- he would be designated the overall political leader for the effort. This really wasn't a surprise to any of us, given his reputation and activities- both in Cuba and Miami. He had been physician in Cuba, and was also a professor at the Havana Military Academy. In Cuba he had been an outspoken public critic of the Batista regime, arrested twice for his anti-Batista activities. Shortly before the abdication of the regime, he actually joined Castro's fighters. Then, after Batista had been removed, Artime was rewarded for his service to Castro by being promoted to Captain, and asked to run the important Agrarian Reform Administration in Oriente Province. But, once he learned what Castro was really about he took asylum- first with the Jesuits, who smuggled him, hidden in one of their robes into Havana, and then on to the American embassy. Eventually, the CIA clandestinely arranged for him to travel to the US on a Honduran freighter. Once in Miami he became known as the leader and spokesman for, a group of former military officers planning to overthrow Castro. He was also widely known to be the head of recruitment in Miami for Cuban exiles willing to participate in an invasion of Cuba. As I learned later, almost all of the officers who were in the Miami group trying to overthrow Castro had once been cadets at the military academy where Artime had taught. Nine of these officers had come with him to Useppa. He and these officers were there when Juan and I arrived. They flew to Panama shortly before we left the island.

Among this group of officers were the San Roman brothers, Jose 'Pepe', and Roberto. Pepe had graduated from the Cuban Military Academy with honors. Once he joined the Cuban Army he had been quickly identified as someone with potential, and was dispatched to the United States for further military training. After he returned to Cuba he was put in command of an infantry unit, and sent into the fighting against the guerilla army. But, in the field he quickly developed an intense aversion towards many of Batista's other military officers for how they routinely abused the civilian population. Following this service he was appointed professor at the Military Academy, and promoted to the rank of Lieutenant Colonel. However, only shortly afterwards he was arrested, accused of conspiring against the state, and imprisoned. But, once Castro assumed power he was freed, and made part of the commission to cleanse the Armed Forces of undesirable Batista loyalists. However, within a few months he himself was arrested, accused of having helped a former Army colleague flee to the United States. Shortly afterwards, he, too, escaped and fled for the states. The high respect with which he was held by his fellow officers resulted in him being selected as the overall military head of the invasion. His steady, professional leadership qualities, tempered by an inherent goodness, made this selection popular within the Brigade. His performance over the next ten months, and on the beach in Cuba, proved that this that this had been a very appropriate and wise selection. Pepe's brother, Roberto, was also good man. Eventually, he became the commander of the Brigade's heavy weapons battalion. He did his part, as well.

Erneido Oliva, and Alejandro del Valle had also come with Artime. Oliva was soon named the Brigade's Deputy Commander. His no-nonsense approach, impressive military bearing, experience in the Cuban Army, and leadership abilities made him immensely popular with the Brigade, too. He eventually led the two battalions that invaded the town of Playa Larga. Alejandro del Valle would command the Brigade's 1st Division- the very elite, highly trained, paratroop unit. Both of these men were true heroes.

All of these, and others, were with us on Useppa. Later I understood that they were on the island to help evaluate us, although from what I saw they went through the tests and evaluations just like the rest. They never acted like they were to be our commanders, or superiors. They behaved as if they were just one of us. But, still, there is no doubt in my mind that everyone there was being evaluated, observed, vetted, and tested. The CIA wanted to ensure that we all measured up to serve in the Brigade that we believed would eventually free Cuba."

"Ernie," I said, "I had no idea that the overall leaders of the entire effort were there on Useppa. It must have been quite an honor for you and your friend to have been included in this group. Had you known these men before you met them on the island?"

"No- neither of us had. At first we wondered why *we* were there- we hadn't had any military training, or experience. But, soon we discovered that many others on the island were just like us- most were really not much more than kids. But, what we all had in common was a deep dislike of Castro, a passionate love for Cuba, a good education, a willingness to fight, and, importantly, we had all come from well respected families. Apparently, that was enough."

"So do I understand you to say that the guys on Useppa never got any real military training there?" I asked.

"We got a little. But, I never really knew if this was just another form of testing, or if was done just to keep us from getting bored. After we had passed enough lie detector tests to make everyone comfortable we began to receive some training on firearms, tactics, map reading, radio communication- that type of stuff. It was all pretty basic, but ultimately it was useful."

"Ernie," Doc enquired, "I know that you didn't know then where you were, but did you ever learn why Useppa was selected by the CIA as a training site for this group?"

"Yes. But, I only learned what I'm about to tell you much, much later. First, let me back us up a little. From what I've been told the idea to overthrow Castro took root in the early days of 1960, almost as soon as Castro's links to the Soviets became apparent. Really, I guess, immediately after Castro had nationalized the American-owned oil refineries and other businesses that were on the island. You have to remember that this all took place very much in the middle of the 'Cold War.' The idea of Nikita Khrushchev having an armed ally, in essence an extension of the 'Iron Curtain,' within ninety miles of the US did not sit well with either President Eisenhower, or with Allen Dulles, the long-time head of the CIA. But, still, this was in the height of the nuclear age- a true full scale direct invasion of the island by the US Marines would risk atomic retaliation by the Russians. It was a risk that Eisenhower and Dulles knew that they could not afford to take. But, doing nothing was not an option, either. Together they decided on a middle road- a 'covert' plan of action to unseat Castro and his regime. For the previous fifteen years, since the end of the Second World War, the United States and the Soviet Union had lived by an unwritten agreement that both sides would try to avoid a direct clash, and that 'covert' actions, cloaked behind 'plausible deniability,' would not be the basis for confrontation. This had worked elsewhere in the Caribbean. In 1954 the US had done exactly the same thing in Guatemala- overthrowing the democratically elected government there after it had started to seize land that belonged to the United Fruit Company. Early in 1960, Eisenhower concluded that something would have to be done about Castro- as evidenced by a speech he gave in which he said, "This nation cannot, and will not, tolerate the establishment of a Soviet satellite ninety miles off our shores." That speech was the green light that the CIA needed to proceed.

Within a few weeks they began establishing bases around the US, and the Caribbean, to assemble, train, equip, and transport a force of Cuban exiles for the express purpose of overthrowing Castro. Initially, it was thought that the CIA would simply need to insert a relatively small group of guerilla exiles into Cuba, and that they would soon be able to incite a revolt sufficient to bring Castro down. But, eventually, events and timing overtook that simple, and possibly naïve, plan. Shortly after Eisenhower had given the green light the CIA established a location in the Florida Keys for training the boat crews that would land the invading force on the beach. In Key West, on a secluded portion of Stock Island, work had begun on converting and equipping the ships needed to transport the invasion force to Cuba. In Louisiana, south of New Orleans, and in Vieques, Puerto Rico, additional bases were established to train Cuban frogmen in the arts of diving, underwater demolition, small arms, and commando training. At the same time a large number of B-26 bombers were sanitized of any identification that could be used to link them back to the US. Dozens of Cuban pilots were trained to fly these, and the other types of aircraft craft that would be needed to protect and resupply the fighters. My cousin Carlos was involved in this effort. In addition, bases for training large number of troops were brought on line in Panama, Guatemala, and Nicaragua. And, of course, hundreds, eventually well over a thousand, volunteer Cuban exiles were recruited to take part in the fight.

But, I digress. Let me get back to your question about Useppa. The CIA had determined early on that they needed a location relatively near to Miami that was remote, but which could also allow limited military training and testing for the leadership of the planned force to overthrow Castro. This location needed to be both close to Miami and able to accommodate, in relative secrecy, up to a hundred individuals for a period of several months. Using whatever resources the CIA uses they identified Useppa Island as being ideal for their purpose. At that time Useppa Island was in a state of disrepair. It had been little used by the Collier family since the patriarch, Baron Collier, had died in 1939. Since then it had been only lightly maintained. It was heavily overgrown, and many of the buildings and docks were in the early stages of the tropical dilapidation inevitable in that climate. But, all of the buildings, the Inn, offices, storerooms, and cabins were still usable. A phone call from the CIA to the long-serving Lee County Sherriff- 'Skag' Thompson- confirmed as much, and further confirmed that the Sherriff's office would gladly assist in providing security for this top secret operation. A short-term lease for the island was quickly signed between the Collier family and an individual by the name of Freddie Goudie. As I understand it, the idea to provide cover for the CIA was that Goudie, and half a dozen others, had contracted with a personnel company to assess the abilities of all the people that were to be sent there. The first contingent of CIA began arriving on the island May 18, 1960. The CIA was certainly not letting any grass grow under its feet. Later, to our dismay, we would all too clearly understand why such rush was necessary. The first Cubans, Artime and the other officers, arrived on June 2nd. Juan and I, and the others, arrived shortly after that."

"Ernie, that is fascinating. So did everyone who was trained on the island eventually fight with the Brigade?"

"For the most part, but a number of the ones that came, maybe a dozen, simply disappeared while I was there. I don't know if they failed the tests, or were sent off on secret assignments within Cuba. But, for whatever reasons, they disappeared, and I have never seen them again. But, eventually, those of us left, were taken, in secret, back to Miami, and then flown directly either to Panama or Guatemala. Juan and I went to Guatemala."

"When was that?" Doc asked.

"The first Cubans flew out on June 22. That group included Artime, Pepe San Roman, and twenty eight trainees who, we later learned, had been designated to participate in special training for the infiltration units.

"And, when did you leave?" Doc continued.

"It wasn't long after that- maybe a week."

"So," Doc said, "you weren't on Useppa long. How long was the island used?"

"The last Cubans left there on July 5."

"Wow. That didn't take very long," I said. "So the CIA was there for less than two months?"

"Jim, I don't know about that. But, I do know that everyone that was eventually involved with the Brigade was off the island by July 5. I've heard that the CIA may have trained people there for other purposes after we left. But, I don't know that for sure. But, as far as it relates to what we did the island was essentially just a place for vetting and testing those of us who would eventually lead the Brigade. As soon as that was over we were through with Useppa, and we moved on to Central American to begin our serious training.

"Ernie, why did they send you to Guatemala?" I asked.

"Jim, some of the testing was done to determine where we would best fit in the organization– you either got assigned to be in be in an Infiltration Unit, or you were assigned to be in the Brigade. I guess Juan and I must have failed the intelligence tests, or something, since we both ended up with the Brigade. But, that was great with us- we didn't want to slither around in the jungle, spying on people- at that time we just wanted to fight- man to man- to free Cuba. But, roughly a third of the unit were flown to Panama where they engaged in training for infiltration, propaganda, and clandestine operations. We saw most of them a few months later when they were relocated to Guatemala for even more training near where we were located. Finally, they, and many others, were inserted into Cuba to conduct clandestine operations, and to provide information back to the CIA. I've only seen a few of them since, because many of them, I'm afraid, died there. You see, if they were discovered by Castro's men, they were usually executed on the spot."

"Ernie," I said, noticing the strain showing on his face, "I know this is tough for you to talk about. If you want to stop I will understand."

"No, Jim. I want to tell you and Doc this story. I know that I won't have many more opportunities to re-live what happened, and to tell others about it. You see, and I recognize that I may be crazy, but despite what eventually happened to us, I still believe in my heart that what we tried to do then was important. I know that it was important to me. Today, most, I'm afraid, have either forgotten, don't care, or worse yet, know only the lies and the cover -up. You and Doc are probably in one of those categories, too, but, at least, you appear to be interested. I hope you are, because I would very much like to continue telling you what really happened."

"Ernie," I said, "I can assure you that right now neither of us have anywhere that we'd rather be than here listening to you talk about this. We want to hear the whole story. But, if you don't mind, before we go any further, let's grab a new round of beers."

With that Ernie sat back in his chair, and took a deep breath. Truthfully, I wanted him to take a break. I had begun to sense that the stress of him reliving this experience had been taking a toll.

"Ernie," I said, as I slowly handed out the icy, condensation covered cans-hoping to distract, for just a moment, his mind from the deaths of his fellow warriors, "I've always been curious about the name for the Brigade. It was called, if I remember correctly, 'Brigada Asalto 2506.' How was that name derived?"

"Jim, that's a good question. Assault Brigade is, of course, simple. But, the number is not so obvious. To explain that you need to understand that before we arrived on Useppa it had been decided that we each needed a serial number. But, the CIA guys knew better than to simply start with the number one because then, if we were ever captured, Castro would know how few men were actually in the unit. Therefore, the numbering system actually began at '2500.' Then, once we began training in Guatemala, our unit had its first fatality. We were training on a high cliff, practicing rappelling, when Carlos Rafael Santana Estevez slipped, and fell to his death. His serial number was 2506. We added this number to our unit's name- in his honor."

"Thanks, Ernie, for sharing that. I can understand why it's meaningful." Wanting to change the subject again, I asked, "So, where did you train in Guatemala?"

"Most of the infantry training took place in the Sierra Madre Mountains near the pacific coast. The base was near a town known as Retalhuleu, but its CIA code name was JMTRAX. This actual base was located on a large coffee plantation named 'La Helvetia' owned by a wealthy Guatemalan. It was up in the mountains, and overlooked the town. At first conditions there were horrible. There was no infrastructure, and little housing for the troops. So our first task, remember that at that time there were only about 150 of us, was to build the barracks and training facilities. Initially, that was difficult, there were shortages of everything- building supplies, weapons, food- you name it, we didn't have it. But, soon, conditions began to improve.

While this was going on a CIA- contracted, U.S. Construction Company was also building an airfield there. When it was done there was a 4,800 foot long paved runway, with barracks, warehouses, and supply shops scattered around a main building that served as headquarters. This airbase was given the name JMMADD. The main runway of the field was interesting in that it was built on a slope. One end was 150 feet higher than the other. Consequently, the planes always, regardless of the wind direction, took off downhill, and landed uphill. Carlos told me that this made flying there challenging. But, at least the CIA was able to use it to fly in the supplies that we needed. To provide a cover story for the field the Guatemalan air force used the field during the day for training their pilots."

At this point, Doc spoke up. "All of this was done for just a force of 150 men?"

"That was just at the start. The force was growing all the time as new recruits from Miami joined us. We were up to almost 500 men by the fall. But, after that things started to really change."

"Change in what way?" I asked Ernie.

Apparently, at this point, a decision in Washington was made that the whole concept of the mission needed to change- change from being a small scale guerilla infiltration, to becoming a large scale invasion force. Along with this change came a dramatic shift in the quantity of troops- it wasn't long before we were approaching 2500 men. The base was, also, suddenly flooded with a new type of advisor-instructor. These new Americans wore casual clothes, but their bearing and professionalism clearly marked them as military men. In fact, we soon learned, these were members of the U.S. Army Special Forces- the 'Green Berets.' These guys quickly transformed the whole camp into a disciplined military installation. As soon as they came the quality and intensity of the training dramatically improved. I thought to myself as this began to happen that the U.S. was finally beginning to take this mission more seriously. I knew then, we all knew then, that the U.S. really wanted Castro gone, and would do whatever was necessary to make this happen. We were ecstatic with these changes."

"Ernie," Doc asked, "what do you think led to this change?"

"I believe there were several things. First, the CIA's guerilla infiltrations, and subsequent supply drops, had gone very badly. Secondly, the involvement of the Soviet Union was obviously ramping up. It was clear that they had plans to arm Castro to the teeth with planes, tanks, and whatever else necessary to keep him in power. Consequently, the CIA knew that it couldn't afford to wait for the guerilla insurrection to take hold. It knew that it had to act quickly, or not act at all. And, finally, Eisenhower's term in office was coming to an end. The elections were in November-Nixon or Kennedy would succeed him. Fortunately, both had expressed support in their campaigns for overthrowing Castro. As it turned out, Kennedy, of course, won- helped significantly by his criticism of the Eisenhower administration for having done 'too little, too late' to get rid of Castro. I have been told that Eisenhower personally approved the change in concept, and that President-Elect Kennedy, when briefed, raised no objections."

"Wow!" I said. "That was a dramatic shift. I'm curious, with this many soldiers involved, how was the Brigade organized?"

"Jim, there were seven battalions within the Brigade itself. But, keep in mind that in terms of troops each battalion was only about the size of a company in the U.S. Army. The thought was that once the unit was successfully established ashore in Cuba that each battalion would be reinforced with new recruits to bring it up to full strength. The First Battalion was the paratroop unit; the

Second, Third, Fifth, and Sixth were infantry units; the Fourth was our armored battalion. We also had a heavy weapons battalion. Beyond, this there was our air force unit which had twenty two B-26 bombers, and a significant number of cargo and transport planes to help with resupply once the Brigade was landed."

"Damn, Ernie," Doc exclaimed, "this was a whole lot bigger operation than I ever knew about. I guess I've always been misinformed, because I'd always thought that the Bay of Pigs fiasco was just a bungled landing by a relatively small, rag tag group of exiles who didn't really know what they were doing. But, from what you're telling me that wasn't what the Brigade was like at all."

"Don't blame yourself, Doc, for not understanding. You see, it's not that you didn't do your homework- instead, it's that you have been misled."

"Mislead! By whom?"

With this question I could see a change come over Ernie's face. When he had been telling us his tale his face had been calm, really almost serene, as he had quietly recited this story from the past. But, now I could see that strength had replaced the previously relaxed set in his jaw. His eyebrows had hardened, with a deeper crease having formed between them. And, now, there was no missing a new, cold, steely glint in his eyes. Clearly, what Ernie was about to say next was of importance. Doc and I both sat up to listen even more closely.

"Gentlemen," he began, "you have been, unfortunately, intentionally, misled by your own government- let me correct myself, by our government."

"But, why?" Doc asked.

"You were told lies to protect the reputation of John F. Kennedy," Ernie replied.

"Wait! I've always thought this was totally the CIA's fault!" Doc stated, appearing for the first time to become slightly agitated, and just a little defensive. "Ernie my family was from Boston. We have a great deal of respect for President Kennedy."

"Doc," Ernie began, with a hint of softness returning to his countenance, "I understand that for some John Kennedy is a hero. And, I understand that it is never easy when an ugly truth is revealed about someone that your worship. And, I know about the distress that can come when the very foundation of much of what you believe is shifted. So, I want to warn you, before I continue, that what I'm about to tell you may be painful. And, I want to caution you that what I am about to say may be information that will give you reason to reconsider your very trust in your own government. Are you willing to listen? Or, should we just open another beer, and forget we've ever had this conversation?"

Attempting to lighten the tension, I interjected: "How about a compromise? Let's open another beer, and then let Ernie continue with his story?"

But, my attempt at humor was ill timed. Neither Ernie nor Doc reacted to my suggestion. Instead that looked each other in the eyes. Finally, after what seemed like a minute, Doc spoke, "Ernie, I will listen. One has to always be willing to hear the truth."

Ernie nodded.

Chapter Eighteen

"Doc, what I am about to tell you is the truth. The invasion of Cuba by Brigade 2506 would have, if executed as originally conceived and planned, succeeded in establishing a strong anti-Castro presence in Cuba. Whether this would have eventually led to his overthrow, I can't say. But, the invasion failed, not because it was poorly planned, poorly led, and poorly executed, but rather because John Kennedy, of all people, wanted it to fail. And, a series of decisions that he made in the days preceding the operation ensured that it would.

The first decision that he made that impacted the potential success of the operation was to delay the planned date for the invasion from its originally scheduled date of March 10, 1961. This original date had been carefully chosen by the CIA since it had learned that the Soviet Union planned to begin the delivery of MiG-21 fighters, the latest Stalin Tanks, artillery, anti-aircraft weapons, and heavy mortars on March 15. The initial delivery was to be followed by one or two ships per day after that. Thus, it was critical that the invasion take place before this weaponry was on the island and before Castro's soldiers could be trained on how to employ it. Kennedy was briefed on the plans for the action multiple times in the period between when he was elected and before he was inaugurated. A formal presentation to Kennedy and his staff was made by the CIA on January 28, 1961. He asked the Joint Chiefs of Staff to prepare a formal evaluation of the plan. One week later the JCS evaluation reported the plan had a 'fair' chance of success. But, shortly after this the March 10 invasion date was scrapped after it became apparent that the Kennedy administration was in no hurry to approve it. In fact, it was not until March 11 that Kennedy even called for a formal approval meeting, and at that meeting the plan was formally rejected. It was not rejected- not because it would have failed militarily- but rather, because the fear the State Department had about the amount of heat that it would have to bear once the action took place. So much for taking action before the Russians landed their weapons."

At this point Doc interrupted. "Ernie, I can understand your disappointment about this delay, but to me it simply looks like the new administration was just trying to be careful- you know, trying to not get involved in a potential blunder this early in its first days in office."

"Perhaps. But this was only the first of many decisions by Kennedy that ultimately caused the action to be doomed."

"Continue."

The original plan called for the invasion to take place near the coastal city of Trinidad- ninety miles further to the east. This city of 26,000 inhabitants was, at that time, a hot bed of anti-Castro sentiment. After the invasion, it was expected to provide a couple of thousand eager new recruits. And, this area was perfect for the type of action envisioned by the CIA. It had sand beaches, with no off shore corals; it had an airfield; and there was an excellent deepwater port- just a few miles to the east. In addition, the location was easily defensible, and it bordered the Escambray Mountains which, in the unlikely event that that it should have become necessary, would provide a possible escape option. But, when the Administration reconvened it rejected the 'Trinidad' plan out of hand. Its objection was that the length of the airfield was insufficient to have allowed the plausibility of the cover story about the Brigade's B-26 bombers to have taken off from that field- even though they were actually initially flying out of Nicaragua, and despite the fact that the invasion plan called for extending the airfield the required extra three hundred feet within a few hours after the invasion had come ashore. But, for this reason, the Administration insisted that the invasion site be moved.

The only other location that minimally satisfied the CIA's requirements was the Bahia de Cochinos, and the airfield at Playa Giron. Despite the fact that both the CIA and the Joint Chiefs of

Staff wrote memos explicitly stating that they preferred the Trinidad location the selection of the 'Bay of Pigs' as the invasion site was upheld by Kennedy. Mistake number two."

"Ernie," I said, "what was wrong with the Bay of Pigs?"

"Jim, there were many things that made it a less desirable location. First, it required that our force be split in two. A large village, Playa Larga, sat at the top of the Bay, with a road that connected it to Havana. This would have to be seized, and held, to prevent Castro from attacking from the north. Second, the beaches in front of Playa Giron, where the main invasion was to take place, were fronted by large amounts of coral. We didn't even know if our landing boats would even be able to clear this coral. Third, there were no friendly inhabitants to reinforce the operation. And, finally, there were no possible viable escape options- either we would have to fall back into the sea, or try to wade into the impenetrable Zapata Swamp."

"So, Ernie, are you saying, that this chosen location doomed the operation from the start?"I asked.

"No, Jim, I'm not. While the operation was, in fact, doomed, it was not because of this reason alone. The invasion could have still have succeeded were it not for the next set of blunders by Kennedy and his advisors."

"Ernie, I'm still listening. But, so far my admiration for my President has not been shaken."

"Doc, listen for just a little longer. The whole operation's success was premised on our large group of B-26's destroying Castro's air force before the invasion began. Then, with complete control of the skies established, our planes would be able to land and operate out of the airfield that we had seized. Flying from there our planes would not only be able to prevent Castro's forces from attacking our beachhead and the ships that supplied it; they could also attack his supply depots and other means of waging war. We believed that if the B-26's could operate unopposed for two to three weeks then the majority of the population would become convinced that Castro must, in the end, lose. We knew that the majority of Cubans at that time were sitting on the fence with respect to Castro. But, they would enter into an open effort to overthrow him only when they were convinced that such an effort would succeed. The B-26 bombing campaign was clearly essential to the success of every aspect of our whole effort. Without complete control of the skies Castro's planes would quickly decimate our landing parties, and sink our resupply ships. And, unfortunately, that is what eventually happened."

"So your B-26's were not able to destroy Castro's planes?" Doc asked.

"Doc, it wasn't that they were not able. Rather, it was that they were not allowed to. The plan called for the Brigade's planes to strike Castro's airfields at dawn, on the morning of the invasion, with our twenty two B-26s. This raid was to be carried out from Puerto Cabezas airfield in Nicaragua, and was scheduled to strike all the airfields simultaneously. In addition, several of the planes were assigned to strike the mass of tanks, trucks, and artillery that Castro had parked in long parallel lines on the outskirts of Havana. We knew that dropping a heavy load of bombs and napalm on this target would have wiped out most of Castro's armor in one strike. After these attacks the B-26's would return to Puerto Cabezas, rearm and refuel, and return to strike the same targets again, along with any of Castro's forces moving toward the invasion beachhead. After the second strike the planes, rather than returning to Nicaragua, would land at the airfield on the beachhead, and commence further operations from there. The next morning, in addition to striking any of Castro's forces around the beachhead and on the highways of Cuba, they would begin an interdiction campaign against key bridges and highway choke points. Then, they would strike the electric power plants of the island, the refineries, and the fuel storage areas. We knew that without fuel and power the Cuban economy would quickly grind to a halt, and the psychological effect on the Cuban population would have been immense.

Another reason why the air operation was so critical is that the invasion plan called for two parachute drops to open the attack at H-hour. These troops were to seize the roads that led to the beachhead. But, without control of the sky these paratroop operations would have been jeopardized. And, as it turned out, they very much were.

"Okay, so what happened? Why were the planes not allowed to fly their missions?"

"Initially, the State Department objected to the number of planes designated to fly the missions. It felt that a strike of this size would have too obviously indicated U.S. backing, and, consequently, was 'politically unsafe.' Then the State Department insisted that a cover story be inserted into the plan. This story would require that the air attacks be blamed on Cuban pilots that had defected to the U.S. To separate this cover-story from the invasion, the 'defecting pilot' raids would have to take place two days prior to the landings! The number of attacking planes was also to be reduced- at first, from twenty two to sixteen. But, the number of raids were increased- now there would be a total of five raids: the first and second on D-2; the third and forth on D-1, and the last would strike on D-Day, six hours after the brigade was ashore. As I mentioned before, the planes engaged in this last attack would not return to Nicaragua, but rather would land at the Giron airfield where waiting ground crews would rearm and refuel them for continued attacks throughout the day."

"Ernie, I'm no military guy, but those changes don't really sound that significant. Five attacks by sixteen planes would have still have meant eighty sorties. If I heard you right, that's more than the initial plan."

"Doc, I agree- if they had been allowed to take place. On April 12, Kennedy held a press conference during which he committed that under no circumstances would U.S. armed forces be committed in any manner in Cuba. Then, on April 14, the day before the first strikes were to take place, the State Department persuaded the President to reduce the number of planes from sixteen to six. Further, it requested that the scheduled follow up attacks after D-2 be canceled all together. So, now, rather than having eighty sorties, we were only going to have a handful! This decision was made just two days before the landing was to take place! Our transport ships had already sailed. According to the State Department these cuts were necessitated to preserve the 'noninvolvement image' of the United States. Kennedy approved these cuts without consulting with either the CIA, or the Joint Chiefs of Staff. In addition, the State department ordered that the Brigade's planes could not deploy the napalm that it had planned to use to destroy Castro's conveniently lined up tanks and guns. Consequently, now neither Castro's air force, nor his army's equipment, would be destroyed. From that point forward, the fate of the invasion force was sealed."

"Damn, I can understand that. But, why didn't Kennedy just call off the whole invasion at that point? It seems to me like that would have been the reasonable thing to do."

"Indeed- one would think so. But, I've been told that Kennedy felt he was caught in a dilemma. During his campaign he had publicly promised to support the Cuban exiles in their fight against Castro. He had even belittled the Eisenhower administration, and by extension- Richard Nixon- for doing 'too little, too late.' But, once he took office he discovered much to his dismay that Eisenhower had not, in fact, been doing little. Rather the General had created a whole brigade of Cubans who ready to fight and die for the freedom of their island. I later learned that in the many meetings in which Kennedy and his staff discussed the planning and approval for the invasion the President and his top staff had actually frequently questioned whether they should scrap the plan and disband the Brigade. But, ultimately, they decided that any decision to disband the Brigade would create additional problems- you see, we Cubans, by and large, had believed his campaign promises. Disbanding the Brigade would cause the Cubans to naturally feel that they had been let down by his Administration, that he in fact had reneged on his campaign promises to them. But, neither did he feel that he could give the

Brigade the authorizations, and support, that it needed to succeed. In the end, he decided to take the easy way out, telling his subordinates that 'the easiest thing might be to let the Cubans go where they yearned to go- to Cuba.' After that, according to my sources, he turned the meeting to consideration of how this could be done. Eventually, he told his staff that 'If we have to get rid of these men, it is better to dump them in Cuba than in the United States, especially if that is where they want to go.' Our ships were already approaching the shore of Cuba when he uttered those words. We were all, in fact, actually being dumped into Castro's lap. It was better for him to have the opportunity to slaughter us than for Kennedy to have to face us and acknowledge what he had done."

"Ernie," Doc said, "if what you have said is true, that's pretty damning. But, I don't understand how you would know any of this. You, I suppose, were on a ship in the Caribbean, getting ready to invade Cuba. How would you know any of what Kennedy was doing, or said?"

"Doc that is a very good question. I was, as you suggested, on board my ship, readying my troops, and saying my prayers. I learned all of this much later, after I had escaped from Cuba, and returned to the U.S. Eventually, I had become employed, as had many of the exiles who were able to return, by the CIA in Miami. I eventually came to know well many who had been involved in what had taken place. They gave me their firsthand accounts. This is the source for what I have told you. That is why what I am telling you is what I believe to be the truth."

"Ernie, if you don't mind telling me, how did you escape the Bay of Pigs? Were you captured?"

"No, Jim, I was one of the relatively few who were not captured, or killed. After I had crawled into the swamp I eventually found sixteen others who had escaped there also. Over the next several days we crawled, moving at night, to the eastern end of the Bay. There we stole a small sail boat- it was only about sixteen feet long. That night we sailed south into the Caribbean, using the stars to steer. Then we worked our way around the western tip of Cuba, before turning north towards what we hoped would eventually be the U.S. It was not an easy trip. Over the next ten days, seven who were with us died. The rest of us were very near death. We were finally rescued by an American freighter still over a hundred miles south of New Orleans. After we recovered we made our way back to Miami."

"Ernie," Doc said. "I can't imagine what you and the others went through. I want you to know that I'm sorry. And, I also want you to know that what you have told me today has led me to, at least, reconsider my prior admiration for John Kennedy. I appreciate you telling us this. And, you are right that not many of us know about this part of the story. But, if you don't mind me asking, how many men were lost at the Bay of Pigs?"

"We had sailed from Nicaragua with almost 1,334 men, plus there were an additional 177 airborne paratroops. Of this number, a total of 114 were either killed in action or drowned. One thousand, one hundred eighty three were captured. Only a few managed to escape."

"Ernie," I asked, "how long were those captured held by Castro?"

"Twenty months, and from what I've been told, those were twenty months in hell."

"I can imagine. Why were they released at all?"

"Eventually the State Department, in an all too transparent attempt to win back the sympathy of Cuban voters, arranged with Castro to release the prisoners in exchange for $53 million- money 'officially' donated by private sympathizers. On December 29, 1962 Kennedy and his wife hosted a welcome back ceremony at the Orange Bowl in Miami for the returning prisoners. Fortunately, I had somewhere else to be that day."

"Ernie," Doc said, "why do you say that?"

"Because, otherwise, I probably would have done something that I would have later regretted."

"So, you were unhappy when Kennedy later was assassinated?" Doc asked.

"I didn't say that."

With that shocking statement a silence descended on the group. After a few moments I once again tried to break the ice with, "Does anyone want a beer now?"

I was glad that both Doc and Ernie raised their hands.

As I passed out the chilled cans I asked Ernie, "Have you been back to Useppa since you left in 1961?"

Yes. Actually, I've been back many times. Twice we've had official reunions of the island for the surviving Brigade members who trained there. But, I also know well that fellow that now runs the island. He and I used to sail together- back when we were younger. Sometimes, when I'm feeling nostalgic, I call him up and he lets me spend time on the island. I'm actually going tomorrow to visit again. Would either of you like to go with me?"

Doc replied that while he would very much like to he had already committed to taking his wife to her doctor's office for a procedure. I, on the other hand, replied that I'd love to go to the island.

"How are we going to get there?" I asked

"I usually just take the noon ferry- along with all the tourists that go to the island for lunch," Ernie replied.

"What if I picked you up in my boat? We could meet at Tarpon Lodge's dock?"

"Jim that would be wonderful. Could we meet at ten in the morning? That would give us time to see the island, and allow us to begin lunch at the Inn before the tourists show up. After that we could make a stop at the museum. There's an exhibit there on the Brigade that I'd like you to see."

129

"Ten o'clock it is. Can we please stop talking now, and just enjoy the damn beer?"

Chapter Nineteen

Useppa Island, located near the northern end of Pine Island Sound, lies roughly in the middle of a group of many islands. To the northwest is the now deserted Punta Blanca. The lovely, and renowned, Cabbage Key, is close by, only a couple of hundred yards due west. To the north are Mondongo, and Patricio Islands. Mondongo, Spanish for 'pigs' intestines,' is now owned by one of Florida's oldest, and wealthiest, families. Patricio Island is now also deserted, but at one time it was the 'garden island' for the Colliers. Further to the east, across a channel, and close to Pine Island, is Burgess Island, sometimes called Little Bokeelia Island. It was owned for decades by Charles Burgess, the man who invented the dry cell battery. This truly amazing property is now owned by a 'dot com zillionaire.' To the southeast lie Broken Island, Part Island, Black Island, and maybe half a dozen others.

Useppa Island is roughly a mile long, north to south, and less than half a mile across at its widest point. Geologically, it is essentially, like many of the other islands in this grouping, high ground that became separated from the mainland by rising sea level roughly five thousand years ago. There is evidence that, even before it became an island, it was visited by native Indians- possibly as early as eight thousand years ago. After it was separated from the mainland it continued to support Indians who lived, for at least a portion of each year, on the island. Shell middens from this period remain today. This type of seasonal occupation of the island continued well into the Calusa period. But, by the mid-1700s, all of the Calusa people had been either killed, had died of disease, been carried away into slavery, or driven out of the area. The island was essentially deserted until 1784, when Jose Caldez of Cuba began using the island as the base for his seasonal mullet fishing operations. In 1831 one record shows that the island may have then been known as 'Caldez

Island.' But, in 1832, a US Customs Agent was assigned to what was then called 'Josefa Island.'

I had to wonder about this difference in the name. One local legend says that the island was named after the Spanish princess, Joseffa de Mayorga, (daughter of Martin de Mayorga, viceroy of New Spain) who had been captured, along with eleven of her maidens, by the Boca Grande-based pirate Jose Gaspar. The story goes that the island was named in her honor after Gaspar, in a fit of jealous rage, had her (and her lover) beheaded when she refused his advances. The legend says that Joseffa's body was buried by Gaspar on the island, which he then named after her. Gaspar was supposedly killed in 1822, so if he really existed he would have been in the same area, at the same time, as Jose Caldez. In fact, some have wondered if Caldez's real role in the area, rather than simply fishing for mullet, was to smuggle Gaspar's plunder to Havana, and to bring back the supplies he and his crew needed to enjoy their life in Southwest Florida. Today most believe that Jose Gaspar, aka 'Gasparilla,' never really existed, and that the legend was created as nothing more than a marketing ploy in the early 1900's to bring potential investors to the area. It is, however, an undeniable fact that US maps from, at least, the late 1700's used the term 'Gasparilla Island,' and 'Gasparilla Pass' to identify the areas were Gaspar was said to have operated. Were these places named after a pirate? Or, did these names originate with someone else?

Regardless of Caldez' true role, by 1833, this fishing 'rancho' is known to have supported a village with 20 palmetto-thatched huts, and about 60 people. By this time Caldez was close to ninety years old. It is believed that he sailed for Havana, for the last time, in 1835. His schooner, appropriately enough, was named the 'Joseffa.'

The Second Seminole War began that same year. In 1836, Henry Crews, the then local Customs Officer, was killed on the island- ostensibly by Indians. But, to this day rumors persist that he may have actually been murdered by a revengeful Jose Caldez and his men in retribution for Crew's crack down on their smuggling activities. Shortly thereafter the island was abandoned.

For the next several decades the island was only sparsely inhabited. But, in January, 1850 the US Army established on the island the short-lived Fort Casey (named after the Army officer, and Indian Agent, Captain John Casey, who was then in charge of the area). This base supported a garrison of over 100 men, and served primarily as a supply depot for the other Army forts that had been established in the surrounding area. Interestingly, military records from this period refer to the island as 'Giuseppe's Island.' Later charts, in 1863, label the island as 'Useppa.' This fort was abandoned after less than a year. With the advent of the Civil War, the island was occupied sporadically by the US Army as the US attempted to blockade Charlotte Harbor. During this period the island sheltered a number of Union sympathizers who had fled there for protection by the Union forces. But, by 1870 that year's census found only two people living on 'Giuseppe Island.' But, it wouldn't be long before things in the area were to change-dramatically.

In 1885 an angler by the name of W.H. Woods, and his guide Captain John Smith, caught a ninety three pound, five feet-nine inches long, tarpon near what is today St. James City, a small village at the southern end of Pine Island Sound. This catch proved, for the first time, that it was actually possible to fight, and successfully land, a tarpon on a rod and reel. This feat was reported in the April, 1885 issue of 'Forest & Stream' magazine, a nationwide publication. This story created a tarpon fishing frenzy. Almost overnight 'anyone who was anyone' in America wanted to come to Florida to experience the challenge and thrill of catching the legendary "Silver King."

Chicago-based streetcar magnate John Roach acquired Useppa Island in 1894, and built a residence, and hotel, on it in 1896. Apparently, the entrepreneurial Roach had realized the possibilities for an upscale fishing resort located much closer to tarpon-rich Boca Grande Pass, than the *San Carlos Hotel* in distant

St. James City, or the even more remote and extremely rustic *Barracks* at Punta Rassa. He quickly constructed an eastward facing, columned home for his family (today known as the Collier Inn), and a 20 room hotel that, initially, he called *The Tarpon Lodge*. Along with this he had constructed a windmill, and a 35,000 gallon water tank for irrigating the island's groves and flower gardens. Then, just as he had anticipated, his nearly frozen tycoon friends from the north descended on his idyllic island hideaway to share in the joys of this hidden fishing paradise.

In 1900, the island was visited by archaeologist Clarence Moore, whose records indicate that the island was by then again called 'Joseffa.' Some of the names of notable figures who visited the island during this period included the Vanderbilts, Rockefellers, and Rothschilds. Another of Roach's guests was the New York advertising executive, entrepreneur, and soon to be legendary Florida land owner, Baron Collier.

Collier first visited the island in 1906. He absolutely fell in love with it, and with the whole surrounding area. In 1911, he purchased Useppa Island from Roach, and made the island his Florida home. He redesigned *The Tarpon Lodge*, adding a third floor, and changed the name to *The Useppa Inn*. He built a nine-hole golf course, and added sand beaches to the island. He also purchased nearby Punta Blanca Island, and built there a machine shop, shipyard, a school, and staff housing. He turned Patricio Island into a farm, using it to grow fruits and vegetable for his guests. In 1912, Collier established the Izaak Walton Club on Useppa. This fishing club was named for the 17th-century author of *The Compleat Angler*, and was widely regarded at that time as being the most prestigious, and exclusive, fishing club in America. It was also one of the first conservation groups in the country, having initiated the practice of releasing all tarpon caught (except for those to be weighed in for records, or other forms of recognition). By 1918 the island offered 71 guest rooms, and had become an extremely popular destination for Florida visitors. During this period Collier also purchased over a million acres of land elsewhere in Florida. But, shortly thereafter the Great

Depression ravaged his fortune, and along with that his grand plans for his extensive Florida land holdings were crippled. Collier died in 1939. Shortly thereafter the hotel was closed, and fell into disrepair. It was heavily damaged by a hurricane in 1944, and was demolished shortly afterwards.

I was thinking about this history, information that I had Googled the night before, as I steered my boat northward up the Sound. I was looking forward greatly to visiting this legendary island. I knew that today the island was home to an exclusive, private residential club- in other words- you needed an invitation from an island resident to get on it (other than the tour boat which ferried, once a day, a group of tightly supervised diners to the Collier Inn's restaurant for lunch). To this point, I'd never been invited to the island.

But first, before visiting Useppa, I had to pick up Ernie. The channel to Tarpon Lodge lies to the east of Useppa Island. To reach it you need to turn away from what is now the Intercoastal Waterway, between markers 50 and 52, and follow the deep water cut (that in Collier's day was the main shipping route) that runs between Useppa and Part Islands. As you approach the northern quadrant of these islands you look for the marker that leads you into the channel to Pineland Marina, taking care to avoid the shallow bank of sand that extends southwards from Broken Island. From this tight entrance the channel leads around the northern end of Part Island, then past Darling Key, and on into the narrow "Wilson Cut." This perfectly straight excavation through the underlying bed rock was dug in 1925, supposedly with the assistance of copious quantities of dynamite, upon the order of Graham Wilson, who then owned the estate that today is known as *Tarpon Lodge*. There are two theories about the labor force employed on this project: one insists that it was dug using only local laborers; another, to me perhaps a more believable tale, says that John L. Lewis, legendary head of the United Mine Workers Union, who owned a home on the island near his friend Wilson, brought down a group of coal miners from West Virginia, who quickly blasted out the channel. Regardless of who built it, I knew that in the evenings, as the sky darkened with the setting sun, I loved to have a drink at Tarpon Lodge, and watch as the boats of fishing guides motored slowly down this cut, their navigation lights dimly glowing as they returned from what had likely been successful fishing expeditions.

But, today, with a bright morning sun overhead, it was my turn to steer up the channel. Somehow it always did my ego good to navigate water with as much history as this place. Looming peacefully behind the Lodge were the tree covered slopes of what had once been towering Calusa Indian mounds. I knew that this was the site of what then had been one of the most important Calusan cities, second only to what is now known as Mound Key, further south in Estero Bay. I always laughed to myself when I remembered that this location had originally been called by the Indians 'Toampe.' Later mapmakers misplaced the name further north- inserting 'Tampa' on their charts at the similarly shaped area one hundred miles to the north.

The Calusa were an advanced and fierce tribe. I knew that they had managed to create a network of canals across much of Southwest Florida. The one on Pine Island was over three miles long, and forty feet wide. Similar canals have been discovered in what is now Ft. Myers. It is believed that some of these water ways even led as far as Lake Okeechobee. It is mind boggling today to imagine how much effort was required, in those pre-construction equipment days, to dig these transportation arteries.

And, as evidence of their fighting ability the tribe convincingly defeated Ponce de Leon's colonizing force in battle at the northern tip of Estero Island. This near slaughter is memorialized by the name given to the bordering body of water- Matanzas Pass. Ponce de Leon himself was wounded by a poisoned arrow in this battle, and he would later die in Havana from his wound. But, this Calusa success was to be short lived.

The Spanish kept returning- their supposed goal was to convert the natives to Christianity. But, the Indians were perfectly happy with their own religion, and wanted no part of this conversion.

For years they resisted. For the Spanish it was a case of 'convert, or be killed.' For the Calusa it was- 'kill, or be converted.' But, as heroic as these natives were, the one thing that the Calusa could not resist were the infectious diseases that the missionaries brought with them from the Old World- the Calusa simply had no immunity to these illnesses. By 1700, due to the ravages of disease, and because of subsequent attacks by marauding Creek and Yamassee tribes from the north, the Calusa were essentially finished as a people. Finally, the last surviving King, and his remaining 250 followers, arranged to be transported by the Spanish to Havana. Unfortunately, it is said that almost all of them died shortly after arriving there.

As I idled up the narrow cut I couldn't help but be saddened by this history. I told myself to at least try to honor their memories by steering as skillfully as I could towards their one time home. But, as I neared the Lodge's dock my mood was lightened by the smiling face of my elderly Cuban friend, Ernie.

"Buenos dios, amigo!" I heard him call as I gently slid the boat next to the dock.

"Buenos dios, to you, too, sir!" I replied, nearly exhausting in the process my entire Spanish vocabulary.

"Senor Story, I am impressed. You have arrived precisely three minutes before our scheduled time for departure."

"Not bad for a little bit of 'dead reckoning?" I asked. "And, I, too, am impressed that you are standing on the dock waiting for me to arrive. That's always the mark of a good sailor."

"As they say, Jim, 'Time and tide waits for no one.'"

"And, not only are we on time, but we've also got plenty of water in the bay this morning. Hop on board."

Ernie carefully, but gracefully, stepped from the dock onto the rail of the boat, balancing himself with one hand against the T-top's frame. He quickly joined me at the leaning post.

"Jim, you have a very nice boat. Do you like it?"

"I like it very much, Ernie. It's not the fanciest, or the most expensive, boat in the Sound. But, it does what it is supposed to do."

"Jim, I'm very glad to hear that."

I looked at him quizzically before asking "Why are you glad about that?"

He smiled broadly, and laughed, before answering "I'm glad you like it because I designed the hull for this boat!"

"You designed this hull?"

"Actually, I designed the mold that was used to make this hull, and to make many other similar hulls for other brands of boats around Florida. Not many know that making the hull mold is the most difficult, and most expensive, part of building a boat. For that reason many builders use the same pre-constructed mold as the basis for their boats. The rest of what they add on is, in my view, just window dressing. But, I digress, that story came from my previous life as a marine architect. I'm just glad now that you are happy with the finished product."

"I'm very pleased. Just give me a minute to clear the cut, and then hold on. I'll show you how she performs!"

I shoved us off, and we were underway. Moments later, as we slid around the shallow southern tip of the Broken Island shoal, I made a point of traveling slightly faster than I normally might have just to show Ernie how well the boat handled. As I did that I could see an intelligent look of concentrated evaluation on his face. But, I thought that I could also see a slight smile. As the boat straightened out onto a plane, Ernie gave me a thumbs-up. Within minutes we were idling into the marked entrance channel on the western side of Useppa. As I steered Ernie asked if he could use the radio to make the arrangements for dockage. I, of course, said yes.

I watched as he twisted the knob on the radio to Channel 14. I had read on the sign at the entrance that this was the radio channel monitored by the Dock Master. Then, I listened in surprise as Ernie spoke into the microphone in his quiet deep voice, not using English, but instead a rich, melodic, rapid Spanish dialogue. I couldn't imagine what the Cracker on the other end of the line was likely to do with that. I raised my head to hear the reply.

What I heard was, surprisingly, also in Spanish. But, while I could understand little of what was being communicated, I assumed, from the tone of the response, that the Dock Master was delighted that Senor Valdez and I were approaching his dock. Quickly, Ernie responded, again in Spanish. The only word I understood was 'Gracias.'

When he was through, I asked, "All right, Ernie, what did he say? Are we welcome, or not? If so, where does he want us to tie up?"

Ernie laughed. "Of course, we are welcome. That was my great nephew Alvaro that I was speaking with on the radio. He is the son of my nephew Alphonse, who is the son of my cousin Carlos. I like to think that I had a hand in helping him secure his current position here as Master of the Dock."

"You did?" I asked.

"I told you that a good friend of mine runs the island. His name is Frank Upchurch. We'll meet him in a few minutes. Now, look just to the south side of the B Dock, next to the tower. The fellow standing there is Alvaro. He's put us in the premier spot along the whole dock- closest to the bar!" With that Ernie laughed again. It was good to see a sparkle in his eye- it seemed already that this trip was doing him good.

As we motored into the sheltered cove I marveled at the expanse of brightly painted white docks and pilings. A good sized fleet of large yachts could tie up here. But, today, the docks were mostly empty. There were only a couple of nice center console fishing boats tied up on the C Dock, a beautiful sports fisherman was at the end of the B Dock, and a couple of what I presumed to be the resort's own boats were conveniently moored next to the walkway that led from the shore to the B Dock's tower. I wasn't surprised by the scarcity of boats at the docks. The dog days of early fall in Florida will do that. Still, I would bet that even in the height of 'Season' Ernie's connection would have still secured us the best docking spot available. I understood from own experience that it's always good to have friends on the dock.

Moments later I quietly bumped forward the boat alongside the pier where Alvaro was waiting. Ernie expertly tossed the bow mooring line to him. He then quickly secured it with a perfect cleat hitch. As that was going on I backed the stern gently against the dock, and wrapped the aft dock line once around a piling and then back to the boat's stern cleat. With those simple tasks we were securely moored. There was no need for spring lines.

I took a moment to switch off the boat's electronics, and gave the boat a visual once over. I always like to make sure that everything on board is where it should be before I disembark. I removed the ignition key, and stepped forward to help Ernie onto the dock. But, I should have known better. Despite his fragile condition Ernie had already stepped, unassisted, from the gunwale to the dock where I could see him now embracing Alvaro in a Cuban-style bear hug. As I stepped off the boat they were already engaged in conversation- in Spanish. I stood politely aside, waiting for them to finish catching up. It was obvious that they were happy to see each other. As I turned to survey my surroundings I noticed a sturdily built, darkly tanned, man exit the onshore office, and head our way. He looked to me to be in his early seventies. But, despite his age, he appeared to be in good shape. I could see that he walked with confidence, and agility. From that I deduced that not only did this man probably still work every day, but that he was also, likely, the island's boss. This I assumed was Ernie's friend.

That was confirmed a moment later as the quickly approaching fellow stuck out a friendly, but strong, lightly callused hand, and said: "Welcome to Useppa. I'm Frank Upchurch."

We shook hands as I replied, "Nice to meet you, Frank. I'm Jim Story."

"Jim, is this your first time to the island?" Frank asked.

"Sure is. I've always wanted to visit, but I guess I just must not travel in the right circles," I answered, laughing as I said that, trying to make sure he understood that I was putting myself, and not the island, down.

"Well, if you're traveling with Ernie Valdez, you're damn sure traveling in the right circles for me!" With that he turned to where the two relatives were still happily, and obliviously, talking. He then put a strong, large-boned arm around Ernie's shoulder, and said:"Damn, sailor, don't you know the proper way to land on a man's island! You haven't even asked 'permission to come ashore' yet!"

As Frank said this I could see a huge smile immediately spread across Ernie's face. Recognizing the voice that had spoken to him he spun around into Frank's warm embrace- the type of hug that only men who are old, and dear, friends will give each other.

After that hug, they stepped apart, and looked each other in the eyes. Apparently they were both satisfied with what they saw. Then it was Ernie's time to speak, "Forgive me my dear friend. It appears that I have indeed forgotten my manners. Let me introduce you to my friend, from St James City, Jim Story."

"Thank you, Ernie, but we've already met."

"Well, then let me introduce Jim to my nephew. Alvaro, say hello to Jim Story."

"Mr. Story, it is nice to meet you."

"Nice to meet you, too, Alvaro," I said.

"That's a good looking boat you have, Mr. Story."

"Thank you, Alvaro. It's not much when measured by what normally docks here, but still it was very nice of you to say so. Did you know that it was designed by your uncle?"

"No. But, I'm not surprised. According to him he designed the hulls of just about every boat that docks here."

"What do you mean by 'according to him'?" Ernie interjected. "It's true. Almost every hull mold used in the state came first out of my shop."

"I know, Uncle Ernie. I just like to give you a hard time. Jim, welcome again to Useppa. I hope you will enjoy your time here." With those words, he returned to his paid role of Dock Master, turned, and headed towards his awaiting duties on the dock's tower, leaving us alone with Frank.

"Come with me, Gentlemen," Frank commanded. "Let's get out of this damn sun."

He didn't have to ask me twice. The unfiltered rays of a cloudless sky, combined with little wind, and ample humidity, were already taking their toll. My cotton fishing shirt was already feeling damp. A few moments later we were in the air conditioned comfort of Frank's small office. I couldn't help but admire the paneling that lined the walls and ceiling of the entire structure. I had immediately recognized this wood as being the knotted, iron-hard, turpentine-infused, lightard pine that, back when I was a child, was so prevalent in Florida. That kind of wood just isn't around anymore. Now, every time I see it, I'm reminded to be glad that I wasn't the one who had to cut, saw, and plane, that wood. Those men, back in the day, worked a lot harder than we do now.

"Ernie," Frank began. "It really is good to see you. I was hoping that we would be able to get together. I'd heard from our friend Kiko, who came out here last week, that you weren't feeling great. Are you doing okay?"

"Frank, as they say, 'for everyman there is a time, and a place.' I'm afraid that my time is coming. But, I wanted to be able to see this place once more. I very much appreciate you letting me come."

"Any time my friend. Anytime. Now what can I help you with while you are here?"

"I came to set on the bench, under the tree by the pool, and look out at the bay one more time. But, I also want to show Jim around the island. He's never been here. Naturally, I want him to see how beautiful it is. But, I also want to help him imagine how it was back when the Brigade was here. We, of course, will have lunch at the Inn. And, finally, I want us to stop by the Museum. There is some information there that I want him to see- pictures, names, that kind of stuff. My friend, will you be able to join us for lunch?"

"I wish I could be with you, but, unfortunately, I've got to meet a man from the County. You know, the last thing that I want to do is to have to be nice to some 'wet behind the ears' inspector from the mainland who's trying to tell me how to do things out here. But, that is why, I guess, I get paid the big bucks. I'll have Jimmy at the front desk get you a key to a golf cart. Just make sure you get to the Inn before the crowd arrives at noon."

"Don't worry, my friend. We'll make sure that our orders are placed before the ferry even ties up. Frank, it really has been great to see you again. I'll make sure to stop by before we leave."

"It has been good seeing you to, Ernie. Oh, by the way, a guy by the name of Robert Barnes was asking about you the other day. I don't know if you know, but he lives out here now. Somehow, when we were talking yesterday, your name came up. I probably mentioned that you were coming out to reminisce on the island. Anyway, when he learned that you and I were friends, he said that you two went back a long ways, and that he'd love to see you again. Actually, you'll probably run into him at the Inn. He eats lunch there every day- punctually- at noon. He has a standing reservation for the table in the side room, nearest the window that looks over the bay. You may want to look for him."

"So," Ernie replied, "I take it from your description of his punctuality that my friend Robert might still be a bit 'straight laced'?"

"I'll say. That dude even irons his fishing shirts, and his shorts. I accuse him of even spit shining his boat shoes," Frank chuckled.

"That sounds like him," Ernie said. "I'll look for Robert while we're having lunch. Thanks again, Frank. It really means a lot for me to be here."

With that, Frank, in the way of a friend avoiding the embarrassment of any further display of sentimentality, waved us out the door of his office. As we rose to leave, he hollered at the desk clerk next door, "Jimmy, get these fellows a key to a good golf cart- and, make sure it's got a fully charged battery."

As we drove the electric cart away from the office I said, "Frank sure seems like a nice guy. So, ya'll have known each other for a long time?"

"Very long," Ernie replied.

"Was he involved in the Brigade?" I asked.

"No. He was just a kid back then. I got to know him later, really just through my boat building activities. He loved to sail, and so did I. Eventually, he and I sailed around most of the Gulf, and a good part of the Caribbean, together. And, with our families, we spent a lot of time in the Bahamas. He is indeed a good man, and a good friend. I'm glad to see that he is still doing well."

"How about Robert? Was he a sailor, too?"

"No."

I waited for Ernie to offer more information, but when there was none forthcoming I understood that it was time to change the subject.

Chapter Twenty

Since Ernie knew where he was going, I offered to let him drive him drive. But, he deferred. "Jim, if you don't mind, why don't you drive? I'd rather be able to look around, and see what I remember."

"Fine with me, Ernie," I replied. "Just point me in the direction where you want to go."

"Good. Let's start with the path that leads behind the office. Just follow it around to the right, and then on to the south. I'll be your tour guide."

It was immediately apparent why Useppa Island was so popular with its current residents. The white sand path on which we were driving was shaded by a perfect semi-tropical mix of overhanging gumbo limbo, banyan, and palm trees. The temperature under this foliage canopy easily felt ten degrees cooler than the sweltering heat we had experienced standing out in the bright sunshine. Now, it seemed actually comfortable. And, this combination of pleasant temperature, shade, and inviting soft clean sand created a strong urge to kick off my shoes so that I could walk this path like I would have if I was a kid.

Apparently, Ernie must have been having similar thoughts- "pleasant here, isn't it?"

"Sure is," I agreed. It's easy to see why folks like it here. Was it like this when you where first here?"

Ernie chuckled. "Hardly. Then, all the paths were overgrown, and the trees were a mess, you know many had been blown over from the storms. But, other than that, the essence of the place- the sense of quiet isolation you feel here- was the same. Now, you see the building coming up on the right- after you go past it, pull off to the right."

I did as directed. The building we had stopped alongside was obviously very old. It had a pitched tin roof, and white clapboard siding. I noticed two old fashioned wooden windows on each side, and more of the same on the front and back. A simple wooden stair led up to the entrance door. Behind the building was a nearly dilapidated water tank- I guessed that this had been the original tank that had been constructed in 1896 by John Roach.

"This building," Ernie said, "is where I spent my first night on the island. There were about a dozen of us who arrived on the island together. We came over from Bokeelia, still blindfolded, on the island's boat. Of course, it was very late when we arrived- probably, three in the morning. The room was filled with double bunks. We were each given a blanket and a pillow, and told to get some sleep. But, despite how tired we were, that was not easy to do- we were excited about what we were doing. And, of course, none of us had any idea about where we were. We argued about that for almost an hour before we started, one by one, to drift off to sleep. I remember the consensus being that we were located somewhere off of Key West. We didn't know any better for a long time."

"So this is where you stayed while you were on the island?" I asked.

"No. We only were here the first night. The next day we were assigned to various houses- just cabins really- that served as barracks for all of us who were being trained. Lets continue down the path, and I'll show you where I stayed."

As we drove further south I marveled at the beautiful modern houses that lined the western shore of the island. Most were three story stilt homes- all had been build in similar "Old Florida," white clapboard, tin roof architectural style. Each of the houses faced out to the water of the current Inter-coastal water way. While they were all built only a few feet apart it was obvious, from the way each was angled, and from how the windows were positioned, that careful attention had been given to minimizing the impression of actually being sited near a neighbor.

As we continued, Ernie pointed at a path that veered off to the left. Remember this trail. When we come back this is where we'll turn to go to the Collier Inn for lunch. The island museum is up that way, too."

We continued a few hundred yards further before Ernie directed me to stop near another small, older building.

"This was my barrack. It's one of the few that are still here- the others have been torn down to build houses. There's not much for you to see. But, still this is where I spent an important month of my life. I always like to come back here whenever I'm on the island- just to think about those who were here with me. Jim, I'm going to get out of the cart for a few minutes. I like to sit on the bench under that tree and just remember. Why don't you take the cart to explore the rest of the island, and come back to pick me up in about fifteen minutes. Then, we'll go to lunch."

"Sounds like a plan, Ernie."

I steered the cart on down the path, moving slowly. I wanted to give Ernie plenty of time to reflect. Although he hadn't said anything, I understood that this might be the last time that Ernie would have the opportunity to visit the island, and to visit his memories. I wanted this trip to be a good one. When I returned Ernie was sitting on the bench. He was still, his back was straight, his head was high, and his eyes were staring. I couldn't be sure, but I suspected that they were focused somewhere in the past. A couple of minutes later I saw him take a deep breath, exhale, shake his head, stand, and head towards the cart.

When he arrived I asked, "Are you okay?"

"Jim, I'm fine. Thank you for giving me a moment to be with my friends. Now, are you hungry?"

"Ernie, I'm starved."

"Good. Let's go to the Inn. We need to make sure we get seated before the tour boat crowd arrives. I saw it coming up the channel about a minute ago. And, by the way, the food at the Inn is excellent!"

"Ernie," I warned, "okay then- hang on."

The Collier Inn was once the residence for the Collier family. Today it serves as a restaurant, and bed and breakfast for the island. The building sits high on a mound, possibly once an Indian midden. The two story building, like all the others on the island, features white wooden siding, old style wooden windows, and a tin roof. The front of the building faces to the east, overlooking the wide channel between Useppa and Part Islands. I had learned in my research that this deep water had in Collier's days been the area's main boating channel. There is a long, well built, white painted, t-shaped, dock in front of the house. As I walked towards the building with Ernie I couldn't help but wonder about all the famous people who had landed at that dock.

To the left of the path that we were walking on was a large, flat, perfectly manicured, square of lawn that I recognized as the island's famous regulation-sized croquet court. I could see tasteful wooden benches for spectators positioned around the perimeter of the court. Colorful croquet wickets and poles were properly arranged for a match. But, today, being out of season, there was no game in progress. To the right of the path, I noticed, sitting on top of a hill, under the shade of two large trees, a small, square, rusty tin roofed, open, wood-floored, gazebo. I noticed there a couple of unoccupied wicker chairs, arranged perfectly for gazing out over the sound. It looked like a perfect spot to sit and quietly reflect.

Further along this path I saw a full-scale, life-sized, chessboard, constructed with sixty four red, and white, concrete squares. Complete sets of two foot tall, wooden, black and white, chess pieces were arranged on the board, awaiting players willing to stand in the sun and compete. Maybe, in season, I thought. Next, we came to a palm-shaded swimming pool, deck, and yet another shaded gazebo. I noticed that a quartet of young folks were swimming and lounging. As we passed we could overhear them speaking in a language that sounded like German. They, of course, paid no attention to two old men slowly strolling by.

As we approached the building the path passed beneath the spreading branches of a huge ficus. There was an outdoor patio with tables, chairs, and umbrellas. But, it was obvious that they weren't being used today. Maybe, again, in season. The path ended at the side door of the building which was now obviously the main entrance to the restaurant. As we stepped inside it was obvious that this had at one time been the elegant home of a very wealthy family. The rooms were large, the ceilings were high, and the woodwork was exquisite. The walls were currently covered with framed pictures of boats, fishermen and their catches, and beautifully dressed ladies- all from the period when the island was operating at its most exclusive peak. In the entrance room there was a very large mounted tarpon hanging on the wall over the sofa. It was obvious that this mount was an actual taxidermined specimen- not a plastic replica that fishermen have to settle for today. The room that we entered had obviously originally been the main foyer of the house. Two glass-framed, French doors that overlooked the water were positioned to welcome guests as they crossed a shaded porch. To reach this point they would have walked across a patio, after coming up the long dock that was perfectly aligned with the front of the house. Arriving guests would, I'm sure, have been impressed.

As we were led to our table, I noticed that along the wall space above the windows of the gorgeous Izaak Walton Bar were dozens of other fish mounts. I recognized a snook, a redfish, a grouper, and an absolutely huge speckled trout. But, there were many, many more- some of which I couldn't identify.

After we had been seated at a window-front table that overlooked the water, and while we waited for our server, Ernie spoke, "This building is where we were tested. All those rooms in the back, and upstairs, were assigned to the doctors, psychologists, lie detector machine operators, and all the others who were tasked with examining us. I spent a lot of time here as those guys tried to determine what we could do best, while trying to figure out whether we were double agents. My memories of this place are not as pleasant as the ones I have of my barracks, and some of the other places where we trained."

"I'm sorry, Ernie," I said. "If you would prefer to leave we don't have to eat here. We can leave."

"Don't be silly, Jim. Of course, we are going to eat here! The food they serve is excellent. I highly recommend, as an appetizer, a bowl of their conch chowder. I believe it's the best that I've ever had- and I've spent a lot of time in the Bahamas."

"That sounds great," I replied. "I love conch chowder."

Our server arrived at this point. We quickly placed our orders. Ernie asked, appropriately enough I thought, for a Cuban sandwich. I opted for a Grouper Sandwich. We both ordered bowls of chowder.

While we waited for our food I asked Ernie to tell me more about his time on the island. He explained that when the men weren't being evaluated they were trained on radio communication, use of codes, compass navigation, and other types of basic military skills. "Really, I think all of that was more just to keep us busy, and occupied, while they figured out whether they could trust us. Still, we had a lot of time on our hands. As we came up the path to the Inn I'm sure the small gazebo under the trees? I spent a lot time sitting there with my friends- just smoking, talking, arguing, and wondering about what we were getting ourselves into. I have a lot of very fond memories of that place."

"I've never seen you smoke, Ernie. Do you still smoke?"

"No. I've given that up. Now, I never smoke."

"Not even a cigar?" I asked.

"Especially, not a cigar," he answered. "I'd given up cigarettes after the Bay of Pigs. But, I still liked cigars occasionally. My wife had been after me for years to quit. Finally, when she died ten years ago I swore an oath on her grave that I would never again smoke a cigar until I could stand in the middle of Havana's Plaza de la Revolucion, deliver a public toast to the memory of Jose Marti, spit, and yell a curse at the Castro's. So, Jim, that is why I don't smoke cigars. I always keep my promises."

"Perhaps you will still be able to do that, Ernie. Your days aren't over yet."

"Thank you for that, Jim. It was kind of you. But, I no longer hold out hope of being able to do that. My time is very nearly up. You don't know this, but a month- maybe two- is what my doctor is now saying I have left. Cuba is never going to be free by then. But, Jim, please don't feel bad for me. I've been able to do more in my life than most. And, I've actually made a difference in the world. Not many men can say that they were actually able to do that. I've got no regrets."

Feeling curious about what he had just said, I asked, "Ernie, if you don't mind me asking, what was your accomplishment that made a difference in the world?"

Ernie shrugged. "Jim, unfortunately, I can't yet tell you that. But, I've written a book about it. And, it is my intention to have the single copy of that book delivered to the editor of the Ft. Myers News-Press in the last days before my death. I don't want to have to discuss what's in that book while I'm alive. The last thing I want now is to become famous, or infamous, and have to deal with all that goes along with that. And, who knows, I could still be in jeopardy- legal, and otherwise. But, after I'm gone I want the world to know what I, and my friends, did- and, more importantly, why we did it. So, Jim, I'm afraid that only after I'm gone will you be able to know about the accomplishment of which I am most proud."

151

"Ernie thanks for sharing this with me. I'm looking forward to reading about what you did- just not any time soon."

Ernie smiled. "Thank you. Now, here comes our food."

The meal was as good as Ernie had promised. I had to agree that the chowder was the best that I'd ever had. We had just placed an order for Key Lime Pie when we noticed a large noisy group walking around the front of the building, obviously heading for the side entrance.

"That's the tour group," Ernie said. "Thankfully, we're almost done. It will get very loud in here after they come in."

"Yeah. I bet. Did you say that the pie is good?"

"I'll let you be the judge, Jim. Promise to tell me what ......"

Ernie stopped mid-sentence. I could see that he was looking in the direction of an older man who had just entered the building. He was being seated with his back to us at a reserved window-front table in the bar. From his ramrod straight posture, pressed clothes, and polished shoes I deduced that this was probably the aforementioned Robert Barnes.

"Jim, excuse me for a moment. That fellow that just came in is Robert Barnes. I'd like to go say hello. I'll be back shortly."

"Take your time, Ernie. The coffee's good, and the view is great."

I watched as Ernie approached the table where Robert was sitting. As soon as Robert recognized Ernie, he stood up and extended his hand in welcome. But, when Ernie arrived he ignored the hand, and instead wrapped his arms around Robert, and then gave him a manly hug. Clearly, these two did in fact know each other. It also seemed that they held each other in regard. They then seemed to spend a few moments catching up on old times. It looked as if they enjoyed this. But, then, to my surprise, I noticed a cloud of what might have been concern pass over Ernie's face. I saw him quietly motion that Robert should step outside with him. Obviously, what they now needed to say to each other had to be said where no one else could hear.

As I continued to watch they stepped well away from the building, walking partially down the hill, towards the water. There, they begin to talk again. But, this time they did not appear to be enjoying their conversation so much. Initially, it looked as if Ernie was trying to explain and make a point about something to Robert. In response, Robert appeared to express disagreement. I even saw him poke an angry finger into Ernie's chest, as if trying to clearly, and strongly, make a point. Then, as if in conclusion, I saw Ernie respond quietly, calmly, but firmly to Robert. Then, he extended his right palm- clearly, he was asking for a handshake. For a moment I thought that Robert was not going to reciprocate. But, finally Robert shook his hand. Then, they again gave each other a hug, before calmly turning to walk together, side by side, back to the Inn. Ernie politely held the door open for Robert as they entered. But, I noticed that they didn't speak when they separated to walk towards their tables.

Ernie reached our table just as the deserts and coffees were delivered. We ate in silence- I could tell that Ernie no longer seemed eager to chat. But, he did manage to convey a question, just by raising one eyebrow while glancing at my pie, about my thoughts on the quality of the dessert. I told him that it was the best that I'd ever had. He gently shook his head in the affirmative, smiled, and winked one eye to silently indicate his agreement. When the waitress came back to determine whether we wanted coffee refills we both declined. I asked for the check.

A few minutes later we were outside walking on the path that bordered the croquet lawn. We had parked our golf cart at the head of this walkway in a small shell paved parking lot next to another neat white, wooden, tin roofed building. I was beginning to climb aboard the cart when Ernie stopped me.

"Jim, before we go I'd like you to see the museum in this building. It'll only take a few minutes.

We climbed the white painted wooden steps that led to a landing and then the door to the museum. As I opened the door I was pleased with the welcoming wave of cool air that greeted us. If nothing else, the museum's air conditioning system was first class. We were greeted pleasantly by the smiling receptionist/ docent/ gift shop clerk who obviously was in charge. I guessed, since we were the only persons in the museum, that she was likely delighted for some company. It was also obvious that she and Ernie knew each other.

"Mr. Valdez, it is so good to see you, and to have you once again in the museum. It has been far too long since you were last here. We have missed you so much."

"Ah, Gloria, thank you. I have missed your smiling face, too. It is indeed good to be back. My friend Jim Story has come with me to learn about the Brigade. I wanted him to see the pictures and the display. I, of course, also want to see them again."

"Ernie, I understand. Please take as much time as you want."

With that Ernie led me into the quiet stillness of the museum. We passed several interesting displays focused on the geography, and history of the island. I made a note to find a way to come back when I had more time to explore these in depth. But, today, Ernie and I were here to see the section of the museum that was devoted to Brigade 2506. We rounded a corner, and stepped into another small room. The information about the Brigade was displayed in nearly a dozen plaques mounted to the wall. The first item that greeted my eye was a wooden plaque with the Brigade's insignia displayed at its top. I noticed that this featured the Brigade's number, and a white cross that had the traditional Cuban flag draped across it. On either side of this insignia were gold wreaths that encircled the various military components of the Brigade. Below this were several engraved paragraphs.

"This plaque commemorates the formation on May 18, 1960 of a select group of Cuban patriots that would later become the Assault Brigade 2506….." Beneath this were attached small metal golden plaques.

On each of which were listed the name, and military ID number, of all the members of the Brigade that had trained on Useppa. I found Ernie's in the middle.

The next plaque hanging on the wall gave a brief overview of the invasion. At the bottom I read: *"The battle plan suffered from faulty intelligence, ignorance of underwater terrain, bad logistical planning by the CIA, and lack of support to the Cuban patriots. Defeat was inevitable."*

Following plaques displayed the faces, and short biographies, of the key leaders associated with the invasion. Under President John F. Kennedy's display I read: *"... Kennedy canceled the last two air strikes. It was a tragic mistake."*

Other plaques listed the time line of what happened in the invasion. It was not pleasant reading. The final two plaques commemorated what happened after the invasion had been defeated. One of them read: *"Entering the swamps in small groups, it was every man for himself. They had no food, most had no water, and were fortunate to catch insects and snakes for nourishment. The heat was oppressive. Each had their own horrid story of the long days before they were captured and taken to Giron for relocation to prison in Havana."*

Another picture was captioned: *"Castro captured 1,189 men. Most were held in prison at the Principe Castle."* A later photo on the plaque showed the first released prisoners deplaning from an American Airlines plane that had landed at Homestead Air Force Base. Below that was a picture of Brigade Commander Oliva handing to President Kennedy the Brigade's flag that had flown over Giron for three days. The caption notes that 40,000 people had crowded into the Orange Bowl to watch this ceremony. There was no mention about what any of them thought about this reception by the man who had let the Brigade down.

The final words in the display were: *"... the Founding members of the Assault Brigade 2506 are grateful to the people of the Island of Useppa for allowing us to be part of their history and including us in their Museum."*

Ernie said nothing as we moved slowly through the exhibit. I had glanced up at his face several times, but had not gotten any response. My guess was that his thoughts were elsewhere. Now as we reached the final plaque he gently laid his hand on my shoulder. And this time, when I looked into his eyes, I could see moisture. He said quietly, "Jim, thank you for coming with me. Now, if you don't mind, I would like to return home. I am beginning to feel very tired."

Chapter Twenty One

Five minutes later we had said our goodbyes, and were on the boat idling out the entrance channel. As I steered the boat away from the dock I watched as Ernie stared over the stern. It seemed that he was reluctant to release his grip on the Island's beauty and history. And, I suspected, more importantly, he hated to let go of his memories of what he'd done, and whom he'd known, there. I understood, as he surely must have, that this was probably the last time he would visit Useppa. Only when we had reached the end of the slow speed zone, did I dare intrude on whatever it was he had been thinking.

"Ernie," I gently enquired, "are you ready?"

"Oh, Jim, I apologize for being distracted. I should have been paying more attention to what was going on. I'm ready whenever you are."

Despite his assurance, I still checked to ensure that Ernie was braced adequately for the coming acceleration. Only then did I push the boat's throttle lever fully forward. Quickly, the boat was on a fast plane, sliding forward at thirty miles per hour past the northern tip of Useppa. As we cleared the shallows that protruded from the island's shore we banked to the southeast to line up for the approach to the channel for Tarpon Lodge. Minutes later we slowed for Wilson's Cut. Shortly afterwards we tied alongside the resort's dock. I watched absentmindedly as Ernie attempted to step up onto the boat's gunwale. I hadn't been concerned about him doing this since this morning when he had boarded with ease. But, now he was definitely unsteady. I quickly stepped forward to offer him a hand.

"Ernie," I said, as I took my place beside him on the side of the boat's rail, "Let me help you up onto the dock."

Ernie nodded in silent acquiescence to what he seemed to recognize was a reasonable, yet slightly embarrassing, offer. Once he was stabilized on the gunwale, I stepped up onto the dock, and carefully guided and pulled him to that platform. Once there I kept my arm gently on his back, just to make sure that he was, in fact, steady. It was a good thing that I did. I could feel him sway as he turned away from the boat.

"Ernie, let me walk with you to your car?"

"Jim, just please walk with me to the end of the dock. If I can get there without managing to fall into the bay I should be okay to reach the car."

I didn't argue. I knew that it wasn't easy for a proud man to seek assistance. We walked together- slowly. With each careful step Ernie seemed to gain strength. And, by the time we reached the sidewalk he seemed to largely be back to his old self.

"Jim, thank you for your assistance. I don't know what happened back there. But, I fell okay now. I shouldn't have any problem getting home. And, thanks for going with me to Useppa. It meant a lot to me to be able to see it one more time."

"Ernie, it was my pleasure. I appreciate you inviting me. I did enjoy seeing the Island, and learning about The Brigade, very much. Now, are you sure you're okay? I really don't mind helping you get home."

"Jim, seriously, I'm fine. I think it must have just been the sun. But, whatever, I'm okay now. Have a good trip back down the Sound."

With that he turned and walked, steadily, towards his car.

As I idled out the channel I took my phone from its storage spot in the radio locker, and checked for missed calls and messages. I noticed that Jill had been trying to contact me. I returned her call.

"Hey, Babe," I said. "Did you miss me? What's up?"

"I've got dinner set tonight at the house with Jocko. Hal Smith, Gigi, Kenny and Janice, and Doc and Peg are coming, too. I thought you would like to know."

"Alright- you rock, girl! That sounds absolutely perfect. This should give us an excellent opportunity to find out why Jocko was diving on our spot. I'm leaving Tarpon Lodge now. The boat should be on the lift in a little less than an hour."

"Jim, you just be careful. Don't try to go too fast."

"Before I agree to that kind of restriction I need to know if you plan to get in the pool with me when I get back? You know- I could rub your back- and, maybe rub a few other parts, too!"

"Oh, hush Jim. You're just a dirty old man. You've got sex on your mind all the time!"

"I do not have sex on my mind all the time! Well, maybe, just most of the time."

"Whatever! And, just to be clear, the answer is no- I'm not getting into the pool with you. I've got too much to do to get ready for the party tonight. And, I could really use your help setting things up. So, just pour some cold water on your heat stroke-afflicted head, and come on home. We've got work to do."

"Okay," I replied. Although I hadn't really been surprised by her answer, I did try my best to sound disappointed.

All the invited guests arrived within a few minutes of the specified time for cocktails- six o'clock. On Pine Island this is the standard time that parties begin. Everyone's usually thirsty by then, and for most there's really no good reason to delay beginning to drink beyond then. But, the most important reason for beginning to drink this early is that it allows us to go home early and then go to bed. After all, we are old. There is a good

159

reason that the sidewalks (as if we actually have any) in our town roll up at nine.

For the first few minutes all the guests mingled happily-politely hugging as they greeted each other. But, within five minutes the men had separated from the women, and had taken positions near the bar. Then with drinks in hand they had begun exchanging their latest fishing stories. The women, for their parts, were hovering in the general vicinity of the kitchen, glasses of white wine held at the ready. I wasn't sure what they were discussing, but I was pretty sure that it wasn't fishing. The first thirty minutes of the party pleasantly passed in this manner.

Soon Jocko and Hal were engaged in conversation. They both live onboard large catamaran sail boats. But, since they dock on different canals they normally don't have much opportunity to compare notes. I stood discreetly near them, listening with real interest to their yarns. Truthfully, probably like most men, I've always secretly harbored a yearning to also be a live aboard. But, the one time I'd introduced Jill to sailing it had quickly become obvious that she didn't share that same dream. As I listened, Jocko asked Hal about his plans for his upcoming annual sail to Exuma. At this my interest really perked up- Jill and I have spent many weeks happily vacationing in this area. We've always made a point to stay at the charming *Peace and Plenty* hotel in Georgetown. In my mind, without question, this historic inn is the true prototypical "Bahamian Out Island" resort. When staying there we always made sure that our rooms' balconies overlooked the beautiful, clear waters of that village's famous Elizabeth Harbor. During our stays this well protected anchorage, particularly in the fall and spring, was usually filled with yachts of all types, and sizes. Most of the boats then were lying over for a few days or weeks (depending on the weather) during their annual transit to, or from, the Eastern Caribbean. During the winter the harbor was also always filled with boats and boaters, but these sailors were usually simply happy to drop an anchor in the waters of the warm Bahamas. Hal, we'd learned, was usually one of them.

As I listened he was describing the eastward passage he'd made across the Gulf Stream on his most recent trip to the Bahamas. From the stories he was telling about having to dodge fast moving tankers as he crossed the Gulf Stream it had been a harrowing trip. For his part Jocko responded with a story about the time he had dropped hook in the anchorage at Fort Jefferson, in the Dry Tortugas, to avoid an approaching storm. He described how, despite having carefully checked the set of his Danforth anchor before going to sleep, he'd woken in the wee hours of the morning to find his boat only two feet from being impaled on the rusty iron pilings that had once formed the foundation for the Fort's pier. Apparently, during the storm, the boat's anchor, despite having the appropriate amount of scope, had in the wind drug all the way across the harbor's sandy floor. He said that the only reason he woke up to save his boat was because he had subconsciously sensed a slight change in the boat's motion as it neared the threatening pilings. We all marveled at the nearness of that impending disaster.

For my part, I entered the discussion of frightening sailing adventures with a description of the time I'd crewed on a friend's sailboat on a run from Fort Jefferson to Key West. The trip, that we'd hoped would only be an easy overnight hop, had turned into a marine hell as we'd slammed all night into steep ten foot seas created when an un-forecasted gale blowing from the northeast had stacked up the ocean against the Gulf Stream's opposing current. I'd just begun to describe how happy I'd been to see, as the sun had finally come up, the markers that led into Key West's harbor when we heard Jill announce that dinner was served.

We all found our assigned seats. For my part I had the chair at the head of the table. Jill had assigned Jocko, as the guest of honor, to the chair at the opposite end of the table. Prior to the party I had suggested that she do this, reasoning that with this arrangement I would be able to keep a close watch on his face as our planned interrogation took place.

We'd just begun the salad course when Kenny asked Jocko to tell us about his well known interest in diving for lost pirate treasure. He asked Jocko whether he'd ever discovered anything that was interesting, or valuable.

Jocko had pleasantly replied, happily describing several of the interesting finds that he'd recently made in the waters nearby.

Doc followed this up by telling a story that he'd recently heard about how a plane load of gold that had disappeared in the Gulf following Castro's overthrow of Batista. He said that he'd heard (embellishing for the benefit of others at the table) there could have been a billion dollars of gold on this plane. He asked if Jocko knew about this treasure story."

Jocko just shook his head from side to side. But I noticed that he cast his eyes downward as he did this, being sure to avoid eye contact with anyone. But, the mention of a billion dollars of lost gold did its part to liven up the table's conversation. Soon the ladies were describing what they'd do with that much gold. It wasn't long before they started to encourage Doc, Kenny, and I to organize a search for this fortune. For our parts, we pooh-poohed the thought of there even actually being any lost gold.

The conversation died as Jill served the main course. Shortly afterwards, this delicious entree, Jill's famous Lasagna, had been ravenously devoured. The dinner plates were being cleared to make way for dessert when Kenny asked his next question.

"Jocko, I was wondering if you've been diving in the Gulf recently? And, if so, how deep do you dive when you go out there?"

Jocko replied. "No, I've been staying near shore. I haven't been in the Gulf for a couple of months. I don't like to dive any deeper than thirty or forty feet. Why do you ask?"

"Well," Kenny responded calmly, "We saw your boat anchored out there a couple of weeks ago in about a hundred feet of water. It was about forty or fifty miles southeast of the Sanibel Light."

With that Jocko put his wine glass down, and looked Kenny directly in the eyes. He was not smiling. "Kenny, you were mistaken."

"Possibly, but your dog was in the cockpit- he wagged his tail at us as he waited on you to come up from a dive. You weren't out there looking for lost Cuban Gold were you?"

With that statement the room became still. Jocko then stood up, and said: "Excuse me." Without another word he headed for the door. On his way through the kitchen he spoke to Jill. "Thank you for the dinner. But, I've got to be going now."

As the door closed behind him we sat quietly around the table. For a moment no one spoke- we were trying to gather our thoughts about what had just taken place.

Then Hal stood up. It was clear that he was uncomfortable with, and didn't understand, what had just taken place. "Jim, if you don't mind, I think I better be going, too. It's getting late, and I need to go check on my boat."

"Hal," Jill spoke up, "You are not going anywhere without a piece of my peach pie. I'll wrap some up for you."

"Okay- if you insist," Hal replied meekly.

A minute later he'd told everyone goodbye. Jill handed him the pie, and gave him a warm hug to thank him for coming. Then he, too, was out the door.

As soon as he was gone the dam of pent up emotions burst.

"Did you see that?" Kenny asked. "I really called his bluff about diving for the gold. He knew right away that we knew what he'd done. He knew that we knew that he'd stolen Doc's chart, too. He's guilty- there's absolutely no question about it!"

"It looked that way to me, too!" Doc responded.

Looking for a more innocent explanation, Janice wondered, "Maybe, he just didn't like being called a liar."

"He probably didn't!" Kenny laughed. "But, still he knew that we knew he was lying. He's the thief- no question about it. He stole the fucking chart!"

"Kenny," Janice exclaimed. "Watch your mouth. You don't have to talk that way."

"Sorry. But, ya'll saw it, too. That bastard stole Doc's chart. He probably broke into Ernie's house, too. There is no doubt in my mind that he's going after the Cuban Gold. The only question I've got is what are we going to do about it?"

I interrupted, "You know, we were in such a hurry to interrogate Jocko that we didn't even find out if Jocko speaks Spanish! We should have at least done that."

"Jim, I'm sorry," Kenny apologized. "I guess I just got too excited thinking about all that money."

At that Peg spoke up. "Guys, we've got to get ourselves a diver. We need to see what's down there. Does anyone know how to dive? Does anyone know anyone who knows how to dive?"

We all shook our heads no. Then, Jill responded, "Sammy knows how to dive."

"Sammy? Who's Sammy," I asked.

"Jim, you know Sammy. She's the lady that does my hair."

I stared at her for a moment with a slightly stunned look before asking, "Do you think she'd go down to take a look for us?"

"I'm sure she'd be happy to. But, she'd probably want her husband Brad to go along."

"Brad? Do you know him? Is he an okay guy?" I asked.

"Oh, sure. He's a commercial guide. He's lived here all his life. He's a good guy," Jill replied.

"What do ya'll think," I asked the other folks at the table. "Would you be okay with Jill asking Sammy and her husband to help us?"

"I guess if they saw anything on the bottom we'd have to share the treasure with them," Gigi stated.

"Only if they decided to tell us about it," Doc replied.

Jill began to reply, apparently planning to defend the integrity of Sammy and Brad, before stopping as she began to comprehend the logic of what Doc had just suggested.

"Well, we've got to do something," Kenny exclaimed. "We can't just let Jocko steal that gold. We can either trust Sammy and Brad, or we can try dropping a Go Pro camera on it. What's it going to be?"

"Will a Go Pro work that deep?" I asked.

"Hell, if I know," Kenny answered.

"Why, don't we just do both?" asked Peg. "I think we're going to need the divers down there. But, the camera will help to keep everyone honest."

"Sounds like a good idea to me," I replied. "Everybody okay with that plan?"

No one objected.

"Jill, you touch base with Sammy tomorrow? But, don't tell her about the gold, at least not until we're out in the boat. I don't want the whole island on top of that spot before we know what's down there."

"So what do I tell her about why we need them to dive?"

Janice responded, "Why don't you tell her that Kenny dropped my new grouper rod overboard, and he's desperate to get it back before I find out its missing?"

"Perfect," Jill answered. "That sounds just like something that Kenny would do."

Chapter Twenty Two

The phone rang at six the next morning. Jill and I were still sleeping. It has been my experience that early morning phone calls almost never bring good news. This one was no different.

"Hello?" I groggily answered.

"Jim, Mike Collins. Sorry to wake you up. But, I need to get your thoughts on something."

"Of course, Mike. But, couldn't this wait to a more reasonable hour?"

He didn't reply to that question, but I could imagine him grimly grinning on the other end of the line, happy to finally be able to repay me for the multiple occasions when I'd called him and disturbed his slumber.

"Jim, I've got bad news. Ernie Valdez is dead. A neighbor says that he's seen you and Doc hanging out with him recently. When was the last time you saw him?"

"Damn! I was with him yesterday. We went out to Useppa together. We had a great day. I dropped him off at Tarpon Lodge at little after two o'clock."

"And, he was okay?"

"Yeah, I guess. He seemed kind of weak when he got off the boat, but a few minutes later he was fine. I even offered to help him get home, but he refused any help. What he die of?"

"Our guess is that he had a heart attack. A neighbor- a commercial fishing guy that gets up early- noticed that Ernie's house lights had been on all night. That worried him. He stopped by the house on his way out to check on him, and knocked on the door. When he didn't get an answer he called us. We went in and found him sitting in his recliner in the living room. It looked like he'd been enjoying a glass of good rum and getting ready to smoke a fine cigar. But, before he could light it up I guess he just kicked off peacefully. Not a bad way to go if you ask me."

"Mike, Ernie didn't smoke cigars," I replied.

"Jim, there was an unlit H. Upman- No. 2 near the ashtray on the table by his chair. It sure looked to me like he'd been getting ready to savor it."

"Mike, Ernie didn't smoke cigars."

"Jim, you're not getting hard of hearing are you? There was a ciga........"

"Mike, damn it! I heard you fine. But, you listen to me. Ernie did not smoke cigars anymore. Just yesterday I offered to smoke one with him. But, he told me that he'd sworn on his wife's grave that he'd never smoke one again until he could do it in the middle of Havana's Revolutionary Square while yelling that the Castro's sucked. He was serious when he said that. I believed him."

"So when did he give them up?" Mike asked.

"Ten years ago- when his wife died," I replied.

"Jim, did you ever go into Ernie's house?" Mike questioned.

"One time- just to help him clean and put away up some dishes."

"Did you take a look around when you were inside?"

"A little. Why?"I asked.

"Jim, if you've got time would you mind driving up here to take a look around the inside of the house. I'd like to get your thoughts about it."

"Mike, I've got nothing to do. Let me brush my teeth. I can be there in twenty minutes. Will that be okay?"

"Yep. See you then. And, please, apologize to Jill for me waking her up."

As I drove up Stringfellow Road I relived the previous day with Ernie. I had really enjoyed it. I had also very much enjoyed getting to know Ernie over the past several weeks. In that short time he'd earned his way far up on my list of the favorite people that I'd ever known. I was really going to miss him. I also hoped that his death wouldn't mean that I'd miss learning more about whatever it was that he was so proud of having accomplished. I doubted that he'd been able to mail the book that he'd talked about to the News Journal. I made a mental note to mention the book to Mike Collins.

Ernie's street was filled with Sherriff's cruisers, and his yard was surrounded with yellow crime scene tape. I didn't like the looks of that. When I identified myself to the deputy controlling access to the yard, I was directed where to park, and told that Lt. Collins was waiting for me inside. But, as I walked up the driveway towards the house, Mike stepped outside to meet me. He was holding an unused sterile gown and shoe covers. As I reached the steps he directed me to put them on before I joined him inside.

"Jim, Ernie's body is already gone to the morgue. Don't worry about that. When you get inside I just want your impression of what you see. You don't have to be specific- just let me know if it looks how you remember it the last time you were inside."

"Got you. Lead the way."

I followed Mike into the house, trying not to look at the empty recliner. Of course, given the way that the brain works, that was the first thing my eyes focused on. I took a deep breath to steady myself, and then began a slow three sixty degree turn. I was trying to take it all in.

"Mike," I said as I completed that revolution, "Something seems a little off. It's just not quite as neat as I remember it."

With that I then stepped in front of the bookcase. Most of the titles were still neatly arranged on the shelves, but I noticed that several were horizontally lying on top of the vertical volumes. This wasn't what I remembered from my previous visit. I reflected this to Mike, and looked around the rest of the living room. At first everything seemed the same as earlier, but upon closer inspection I could see that some of the knick knacks on the shelves were not spaced as evenly as they'd been previously. I mentioned this, and stepped into the kitchen.

The first thing I did was to open the door to the pantry. Immediately, it was obvious that someone other than Ernie had placed the items back into the cabinet. No longer was everything neatly organized into the precise rows that I'd admired before. And, besides that, not all of the items were where they should have been according to the shelves' labels. Then, when I looked into the cabinet where the pots and pans were stored it was clear that they had been placed there without quite the same attention to neatness and organization that I'd observed Ernie use. The spices on the wall racks were no longer all alphabetically arranged- some seemed to have been placed there without regard to that constraint. To me it was clear that someone other than Ernie had been the last to straighten up the kitchen. I told that to Mike.

"Jim, thanks. I kind of had that impression, too. A lot was organized with precision, but other stuff wasn't. That just didn't seem right to me. But, I needed to have it confirmed by someone else. It looked to me like someone might have gone over the whole house looking for something, and then put everything back, hoping that we wouldn't notice. Do you have any idea why anyone would have done that?"

"Mike, all I can tell you is that Ernie told me he'd written a book about something he'd done in the past. He told me that he planned to send it to the Editor of the News Journal before he died. You think that might have been what someone was looking for?"

"Don't know. But, now I'm not so sure that Ernie actually died of a heart attack. I'm going to order that an enhanced forensic autopsy is done before we sign off on this. Jim, do you have any other ideas about what might have happened?"

"Just that Ernie mentioned something a couple of weeks ago about there might be a puzzle of some sort on the old chart that was stolen. But, he didn't want us to know any more about it. I got the impression that he didn't want to put us in harm's way. And, Mike, I've got to tell you that I'm absolutely convinced that Jocko Smith has something to do with this." I went on to tell Collins about the events at the dinner the previous night.

"That's interesting, for sure," he replied. "Look, Jim, there's no reason for you to have to stay around any longer. I really appreciate your help. Now, we can handle it from here. But, until we get this wrapped up, you and Jill need to be careful, and try, for once, to stay out of trouble."

"Mike, don't worry about us. I've made a promise to Jill that we are not going to get involved in anything dangerous- ever again. And, I mean it. But, I'd appreciate it if you'd keep me posted on what you turn up. Ernie was a friend."

"I understand. Take care, Jim."

Chapter Twenty Three

As I headed south I dialed Jill, using the car's Blue Tooth.

"What's up?" she answered.

"You're not going to believe this, but Mike Collins is worried that Ernie might have been murdered!"

"Murdered! What happened?"

"He's not sure yet. He wants an enhanced autopsy performed. But, he warned us to be careful, and not to get involved."

"Well, he doesn't have to worry about me. Now, you come on home, and try to stay out of trouble. I'll have some breakfast for you."

"That sounds good! I'll be there in about fifteen minutes. Love you."

"I love you, too, Babe."

As soon as I clicked off I called Doc.

"Good morning, Captain," he answered. "You want to go fishing?"

"Doc, I've got some bad news for you. It looks like Ernie might have been murdered last night!"

"Holy Crap!" he responded. "What happened?"

"Collins isn't sure yet. He's waiting on the results of an autopsy to confirm that it wasn't just a heart attack.

"Shit, Jim! I really liked Ernie- I liked him a lot. Who does Collins think might have killed him?"

"At this point, he has no idea. But, he warned us to be careful. I think you, Kenny and I ought to get together to talk this through. You free for lunch?"

"Yeah."

"Doc, I'll call Kenny. Let's meet at Low Key at noon."

"All right, Jim. See you then."

As I opened the door into the kitchen Jill's worried face greeted me.

"Jim, why does this keep happening to us?" she asked.

"Baby, I don't know, but this time we're not going to get involved. I promise."

"Jim, really, we do need to stay out of this. If someone actually murdered Ernie, than that means this is serious. We need to be careful."

"I agree, Baby. We can't get involved in this."

Jill had prepared scrambled eggs with cheese, and had heated up several "brown and serve" sausage patties. As I dished this up she pulled a couple of pieces of buttered toast from the oven. We took the plates filled with the food, and two cups of coffee, to the small table on the screened porch where she'd laid out napkins, silverware and condiments. Eating on the porch was one of our favorite things to do. With 'no-see-um proof' screens surrounding us it always felt as if we were pleasantly dining in the tree tops that bordered the second-story porch. It always reminded me why we had moved to this sub-tropical island paradise. For some reason, it also always reminded me of just how much I loved my wife. I guess it was because that her beauty so naturally complimented the surrounding blossoms, swaying fronds, and singing birds. Adam, I thought, probably felt the same way about Eve as they enjoyed their breakfasts in Eden. I didn't want anything to disrupt or disturb this sense of peace and contentment.

After we'd finished, we returned the dishes to the kitchen. I was happily washing them when Jill reminded me that I'd promised her that I'd clean the pool deck.

"Not a problem, Babe," I replied. "I can get it done this morning before I meet Doc and Kenny for lunch."

"Why are you meeting them, Jim?"Jill asked.

"I just want to tell them about Ernie, I replied cautiously."

"Well, ya'll just be careful. None of you need to get in the middle of this."

"Jill, you don't have to worry about us."

Before I returned to my work in the sink I noticed what might have been a slightly skeptical look move across her face. But, before I could confirm this impression she disappeared down the stairs- probably to check on a load of laundry.

I arrived at the Low Key Tiki precisely at noon. I noticed Doc's truck already in the parking lot. As I walked through the palm trees that guarded the dining area's perimeter I could see that he had staked out a table that was sufficiently distant to allow us to converse without undue concern about anyone overhearing.

"Morning, Doc," I quietly said as I sat down.

"Good morning, Jim. How are you doing?"

"I'm okay, I guess. But, that was bad news about Ernie."

Before Doc could reply we noticed Kenny sliding his golf cart to a rambunctious stop in a narrow gravel-paved parking slot reserved for such vehicles. He had hardly stepped from the cart before he was engaged in an exchange of mildly insulting but yet harmless pleasantries with several men seated on stools at the nearby bar. Apparently, they had observed, and commented on, his driving ability. Before he reached our table everyone in the establishment was aware that Kenny had arrived. Subtlety is not one of his strongest suites.

"Good morning, guys!" he bellowed.

"Good morning, Kenny," I replied. "That was quite an arrival you made."

"Oh, that was nothing," Kenny answered. "You should have been here last Thursday night. Then I almost put the darn thing in the canal. But, I've learned now not to do that anymore."

"Denise explained that to you, did she?" Doc enquired.

"Yeah. She certainly did," Kenny laughed. "She wouldn't even let me drive the cart again until yesterday. And, only then if I'd promise to not drive it after I'd been drinking."

"That kind of defeats the purpose of the cart, doesn't it?" I asked.

"Oh, she'll forget about that stipulation in a little bit," Kenny answered. "I'll be coming back for 'happy hour' in no time. Now, what are we drinking?"

"I've got us a pitcher of unsweetened tea, if that's okay," Doc replied.

Kenny grimaced, before replying, "Damn, that's sure enough bad news about Ernie."

"Yeah- for sure," Doc answered. "He was a good guy. Did Jim tell you what happened?"

"Not really. Just that Ernie had died, and that we needed to get together to talk about it. So, Jim, what's up?"

"Well, Collins doesn't know for sure yet, but there is a good chance that Ernie was murdered. He won't know for sure until the autopsy is finished. But, he warned me that we all needed to be careful. I wanted ya'll to know that you need to be careful, too."

"What do we have to be careful about?" Kenny enquired. "What do we have to do with Ernie being killed? I didn't even know the guy."

"Probably nothing," I answered. "But, what if this has to do with the stolen chart and with Batista's missing gold. If it does, we sure don't need to be sticking our noses in the middle of it."

"Jim," Kenny responded, "I ain't scared. Besides, if we assume that we might be getting too close for comfort to whoever stole that darned chart, and that he's trying to eliminate anyone who might know the coordinates of where the gold is located, then we are probably all already in danger- whether we stick our noses further in the middle of it, or not. And, personally, I haven't hit a lottery number in a very long time. I could sure use an extra couple of million dollars right now! We just need to get out there and find that gold before Jocko does."

"Kenny, I'm not going to do it," I answered. "I promised Jill that I was not going to get involved this time."

"Well, Doc?" Kenny asked. "How about you? You up for a little swashbuckling?"

"What do you have in mind, Kenny?" Doc questioned.

"I want us to go fishing this afternoon. But, rather than trying to catch grouper I want you to take us out to those gold coordinates so that I can use my grouper rig to drop my 'GoPro' waterproof camera down to the bottom to take a look at what's down there. If there's nothing, we'll back out, and simply go fishing. But, if there is- well then we'll have to figure out where we go from there. How about it Doc? Are you in?"

"You know that I've never minded going fishing," Doc replied.

"How about you, Jim? Are you in?" Kenny asked.

I stroked my bearded chin, and looked down the canal- I was weighing my alternatives. After a moment, I replied. "No, Kenny, I'm out. I made a promise to Jill."

"So, Jim, that's final? You're out?" Kenny asked.

"Yep. I'm out. If ya'll find something on the bottom it's all yours. I'm out. But, ya'll need to be careful. Real careful. I believe, without a doubt, that someone murdered Ernie. And, whoever did that won't have any compunction about murdering us, either. Ya'll need to take a gun with you."

"Come on, Jim!" Doc said, attempting to lighten the mood with a joke. "We don't need a gun- I've got a shark club on board."

I didn't respond. Instead, I looked him in the eyes, holding my gaze until he acknowledged the seriousness of the matter by looking away. After he'd done that I spoke. "Ya'll do need to be careful. Text me as soon as ya'll are coming back in."

With that I got up from the table, and walked towards my car.
After what had just transpired I really didn't feel like eating lunch.

Chapter Twenty Four

At this point I didn't feel like going home, either. In some way I felt as if I had just let my friends down, and I didn't want Jill to pick up on that vibe. I didn't want her to have to share any of the guilt that was beginning to gnaw at my gut. I knew that she was right in making me promise to not get involved; in not taking any risk that could jeopardize either of our lives. But, something told me that Kenny had been right, too, when he'd said that all of us were already involved, and that all of us were already at risk. I wrestled with this until I decided that I couldn't just do nothing. There had to be something I could do that wouldn't make me to feel like I was breaking my promise to Jill, but something that still might be helpful.

I'd driven all the way through Matlacha, dodging shopping tourists obliviously crossing the road to get to CW Fudge, before the idea finally came to me. Somehow this all had to do with the lost chart. The coordinates for the possible gold were on it- we knew that. But, there were also hundreds of other coordinates on it. Were they all marking fishing spots? Or, did they mark something else? We didn't have the chart, but Jim had loaded the coordinates onto his GPS. Maybe when he got back we could take a look. And, there was something else about that chart that had never made sense to me. Why, I asked, had someone written on the back "A Dummies Guide to Home Repair?" Was this the title of a book? And, if so, what could a book about home improvement possibly have to do with lost gold?

I stewed over this question for a while. I was still driving, part of my brain paying attention to the traffic around me- part of it focused elsewhere. It wasn't until I'd almost reached 'Pondella Road' before it dawned on me that I couldn't remember anything having driven there from Veteran's Expressway. Clearly, I knew that I had to get a grip. I called Jill.

179

"Hey, Babe! How was lunch," she asked.

"Oh, it was okay," I fibbed- something I never, ever did with her. "But, I'm driving into the Cape, now. I need to get something at the Depot. You want me to pick anything up while I'm here?"

"No. But, what do *you* need to pick up?"

"Oh, just some chemicals to clean the pool deck. That's all." The guilt from having now told multiple lies compounding in my conscience.

"Oh, Honey, I thought the pool deck already looked great! I was going to compliment you on what a good job you had done. You sure you need anything else?"

"Yeah, well no, actually, I just need to replace what I used up. It does do a good job."

"Okay- whatever. I'll see you in a little bit. Be careful."

"Jill, I will." I made a mental note to myself to make sure that I stopped by the Home Depot and bought some pool deck cleaner on the way back from the book store.

I walked up to the Help Desk at the large chain book store located on Cleveland Avenue- a little uncomfortable, and feeling slightly out of place, amidst this quiet literary setting.

"Yes, Sir- how may I help you?" asked the smiling young fellow who was minding the kiosk. I was relieved that he seemed to be making an effort to not intimidate me- possibly having deduced from me wearing my 'Pine Island-standard'- stained fishing shirt, frayed canvas shorts, and worn boat shoes that I probably didn't frequent the book store all that often.

"I'm looking for a book…" I began, immediately realizing the stupidity of what I'd just said. "I'm looking for 'A Dummies Guide to Home Repair.' Do you carry that in this store?"

"Just a moment, Sir, I'll look that up for you." He focused on the computer terminal that faced him, and typed in the title- a few seconds later the answer to his query displayed on the screen. He turned to me with a smile- obviously pleased that he'd been able to help.

"Yes, Sir. We do have that title in stock. It's in the Home Improvement Section, Aisle L. Can I help you with anything else?"

"Uh,…. Where's Aisle L?"

"Two rows over, three rows back."

"Thanks."

"My pleasure. Good luck with your project, Sir."

I stared stupidly for a moment, until I was finely able to trace the logic behind the encouragement he'd just offered.

"Thank you," I replied. "I'm definitely going to need it." The clerk, for his part, was probably thinking that "A Dummies Guide" was certainly appropriate for me.

When I returned to the car I took a moment to thumb through the newly purchased paperback. But, look as I might I couldn't find anything in it about finding lost treasure. But, I did find a good hint about what chemicals I should be using to clean my pool deck. It was good that I did because I'd already forgotten that I needed to stop to purchase something to cover up the little fib that I'd told Jill.

When I eventually returned home I proudly showed Jill the gallon of pool deck cleanser that I'd just purchased.

"I've never seen you use that brand before," Jill said. "I thought you were replacing what you used?"

"Oh, I was. But, this is better stuff. I bought it instead."

"Well, that's good, Jim. What's in the Barnes and Noble bag?"

Instantly my mind froze. I'd been found out. But, almost instantly, I was able to recover my composure. "I went by there to get a book on Home Improvement. That's where I got the idea to buy this new type of chemical. It's supposed to be great stuff."

"I've never known you to be so interested in doing things around the house. But, it's good to see this new side of you because there are a lot of things I've noticed that need to be fixed. When can you get started?"

"Uh,… you better let me read the book first."

"Jim, maybe you could just take it one project at a time?"

"Jill, you know that's not how I like to do things. I always want to know everything before I get started."

"I didn't know that, Jim. But, if that's how you prefer to approach doing these things that's okay with me. Just let me know when you're ready to get started."

I sulked away to the garage, looking for an out of the way spot in which to store the newly purchased, unneeded, expensive, super pool deck cleaner- reflecting unhappily as I did on Robert Burn's oft quoted poem about tangled webs and deceit.

Chapter Twenty Five

The afternoon went slowly. I made an attempt to plow through the book on home improvements. But, truthfully, Jill had been right. Trying to read this type of book from cover to cover was torture- it was designed to be read one project at a time. But, now it was too late for that- I was committed. And, bored! I kept staring at the clock on the wall, hoping that my phone would soon alert me that Doc and Kenny were coming up the entrance channel. But, as the hours drug on it was silent. I was now beginning to become worried about them- regretting that I'd not gone with them.

An hour later, I was pacing the room. My imagination had started to run away. Finally, at five o'clock I could take it no longer.

"Jill," I yelled up the stairs, "I'm going over to Doc's. He and Kenny should be home any time now. I want to be there when they come in- just to see if they caught anything."

"Babe, that's fine. Just don't stay too long, and, please, don't have too much to drink! Dinner will be ready about seven."

"You don't have to worry about me. I'll help them clean up the boat while they clean the fish. I'll definitely be home in plenty of time. See you in a little bit."

I pulled the truck up in Doc and Peggy's back yard. Their house was on a corner lot, but faced the side road. This location positioned the canal and boat lift near the main road, Warren Boulevard. I had called Peggy on the phone just to let her know that I would be waiting on the dock for the guys to come it.

As soon as I took a seat in one of the Adirondack chairs under the tiki I heard Peggy coming my way. She, as customary, was bearing two of their renowned, welcoming, frozen Margaritas- one for me, one for her. I wasn't surprised since I knew that they always kept an ample supply of this pre-made alcoholic slush in their freezer. It was a tradition with them to enjoy a cold drink once they'd tied up at the dock- a reward for a successful trip.

"Peggy, thank you so much. There's nothing better on a hot afternoon than one of these. Have you heard from the boys yet?"

"Yeah. Doc texted me a moment ago and said that they'd just gone under the C-Span. Should be here in five minutes."

"Great! Just about enough time for me to finish this before I'll have to go to work cleaning the boat. Did they say how they'd done?" I asked.

Honestly, I was dying of curiosity to know what they'd found on the bottom, if anything. But, I didn't know how much Doc had shared with her about them going out to look for the treasure. I certainly didn't want to get her mad at Doc for not telling her. So instead I just pretended to be concerned about fishing. But, quickly, she let me know that she knew what was going on.

"Doc didn't indicate anything about finding treasure on the bottom. Seriously, Jim, do you think there's something like that out there?"

"Peggy, I think there probably is. Ernie told us that his cousin certainly thought there was, and that his cousin had provided the coordinates."

"So, do you think this treasure has something to do with why Ernie was killed?"

I turned to face her, and looked her in the eyes.

"Peggy, at this point we don't even know for sure that Ernie was murdered. All I know at this point is that Ernie is dead, and that someone stole the chart that marked the location of the treasure. But, I think that there could definitely be a connection between these things. I also think that we all need to be careful-very careful. You know, people do sometimes kill people over lost treasure."

I watched her eyes as she processed what I'd told her. Just then my phone signaled that I'd received a text. I glanced at the screen to see that Kenny had let me know that they had entered the canal.

"That the boys?" Peggy asked.

"Yep. Coming in the canal- be here in a couple of minutes."

"Well, I'd better go get them margaritas. Do you want me to get you a refill?"

"Yeah, you might as well" I replied. "There's no sense in them drinking alone."

"I agree with that line of reasoning," Peggy responded. "I'll be back in a minute."

I watched as Doc's big boat slowly motored up the canal. I studied Kenny's face, but at a distance it gave nothing away. From all I could tell the two boys were simply coming in from an afternoon of fishing. As they approached the dock I hailed them.

"Hey, guys! Ya'll do any good?"

"Nah," Kenny replied. "We struck out- all the way around. Didn't catch a darn thing."

"Dang it," I responded. "That's too bad, and unusual, for you guys!" As I said this I couldn't help but wonder if Kenny was telling me that they hadn't caught fish, or if they hadn't found treasure, or even if they were telling me the truth. After all, I had told them earlier in the day that I was out of the treasure hunting business- and I meant it. But, still….. I really wanted to know if they'd found any treasure.

I watched as Doc calmly, and expertly, idled the big center console onto its lift bunks, positioning it perfectly on his first attempt. The boat had hardly stopped moving before he'd triggered the remote control device that signaled the electric lift motors to raise the craft out of the water. As the boat moved upward Kenny began handing me items that needed to be off loaded. We'd all been fishing together on this boat so often that this exercise was by now well practiced. In fact, by the time the boat stopped moving upward it had been completely unloaded. After I'd lowered onto the dock the big cooler that normally held fish that had been caught I couldn't help but steal a look inside. But, other than a couple of large chunks of ice, it was empty. With that I looked questioningly at both Kenny and Doc.

"Jim, you didn't miss anything" Doc said. "It's been a long time since we've been skunked. We couldn't even catch any snapper."

"That's surprising, Doc. Did ya'll fish that one special spot we talked about?" I asked.

I noticed Doc and Kenny glance quickly at each other. I could then see Kenny nod back, almost imperceptibly.

"Jim, we were out there for hours on that one spot. Truthfully, that's the only spot we fished. But, we didn't find anything."

"What," I asked curiously, "did the electronics show? Could you see anything on the bottom?"

"Nothing. It was flat. From what we could tell there was nothing down there but sand."

"That's too bad," I said. "I guess maybe the coordinates were wrong."

"Yep," Doc replied. "It's a big ocean."

"You've got that right," I replied. "But, at least we don't have any fish to clean."

"Yep. At least there is that," Doc laughed to himself softly.

Just then Peggy returned with a tray bearing four frosty glasses filled with frozen margaritas.

"Ya'll get out of the boat and come over here under the tiki. It looks to me like you need to cool down a bit."

"Oh, bless you, Miss Peg," Kenny exclaimed. "Those sure do look good!"

For the next half hour we all sat around- enjoying the drinks, and chatting. Not wanting to destroy the happy mood I'd delayed asking the other question about which I'd been concerned. But, finally, I had to ask.

"Did, uh, ya'll see anyone else out there while you were fishing?"

Doc answered, "Nope. We didn't see anybody."

"That's good," I said, relieved that nobody had observed them as they'd scoured the bottom.

"Well, almost, nobody," Kenny responded. "I do remember seeing a big commercial fishing boat that passed us, heading in, about a mile off to the west. But, it was probably too far off for anyone to see us, so I don't think it counts."

"Probably not," I agreed. "And, just so you won't think that I wasn't doing anything to help, while ya'll were gone I went into town and bought a copy of that book whose title was written on the back side of Ernie's chart- you remember, "A Dummy's Guide to Home Repair.""

"What the heck are you going to do with that?"Doc asked.

"I don't know. But, I'd like to spend some time in the morning going over your GPS. I want to see if any of the spots that you plotted from Ernie's chart tie back to that book in any way. It's a long shot- but, I don't know what else to do. Ya'll want to help me?"

"Jim, you're welcome to come over. I can help get you started, but Peggy and I have Doctor's appointments in the Cape at ten. After that we've got some shopping to do, so we won't be back until three, or so. How about you, Kenny?"

"No. I'll be tied up, too. I promised to take Janice shopping for floor tiles. She's hot and bothered to redo the floors. You know that she's never been happy after we had water in the house last year from that week long rain storm. So, I'll be tied up most of the day, too."

"It's no big deal, guys. I've got no idea what I'll be looking for. All I know that the title of this book was written on the back of the missing chart. Probably doesn't have any connection at all with the treasure. But, truthfully, at this point, I don't know what else to do."

"Well, Jim, just come on over about eight thirty in the morning. I'll get you oriented on the GPS, and then leave it to you."

"Sounds perfect," I replied. "Now, let's get this boat washed down."

Chapter Twenty Six

Jill was delighted that I'd arrived home early, and relatively sober. We enjoyed dinner, our plates sitting on TV trays as we concentrated on trying to help Pat and Vanna solve the puzzles of yet another episode of "Wheel of Fortune." After that we tried our hand, admittedly less successfully, with "Jeopardy." After we'd cleaned up, we next shivered through a couple of frightening editions of "Deadliest Catch." Another quiet, uneventful, evening on Pine Island. I marveled, as I walked the dogs in preparation for retiring, just how enjoyable it can be to do nothing- as long as you're doing it with the one you love. Then it was time for bed- I was looking forward to a good night of sound sleep. But, unfortunately, restful slumber was not to come.

At three thirty I woke, shaken by what had seemed like hours of struggling through the strangest dream- a dream about trying to use familiar household tools to repair, frustratingly with only limited success, a damaged, decaying airplane- all the while trying to decipher instructions for doing this found in an old, handwritten, leather-bound book that I'd been given, quite inexplicitly, by a wise old grouper who'd swum by. These instructions, however, were written in Spanish (which fortunately, for some weird reason, I was able to read)-but, maddeningly, they seemed to have been disguised in what for me was an indecipherable code. And, to make matters worse, periodically I had to leave my challenging task to hide from a menacing, one-eyed, peg-legged pirate who randomly passed by, armed with a cutlass in one hand and a spear gun in the other. Fortunately for me, to this point, for some unexplainable reason, this buccaneer had not been able to see me, even though his friendly accompanying dog with a happily wagging tail kept sniffing me out. Needless to say, my night had been anything other than restful.

I quietly slipped out of bed, intent on distancing myself from this troubling nightmare. I silently padded into the bathroom, relieved myself, washed my hands, and then splashed a little cold water on my face in an attempt to distance myself from the strenuous efforts I'd been dealing with in my slumber. I considered slipping back into the bed, but knowing that there I'd probably just toss and turn, and fearful that I'd likely wake Jill, I made the decision to slip downstairs to pour myself a comforting glass of milk. The dogs raised their heads as if to enquire whether they were expected to come with me, and both seemed relieved when I whispered "stay" to them. They gladly laid their heads back onto the comfort of their beds.

Once downstairs I opened the refrigerator and took out the milk jug. For a moment I wrestled with the question of whether I should pour a couple of measures of good Scotch whisky into the milk, a practice I'd learned to respect decades earlier from an old banking colleague. But, finally, reasoning that it was already too close to the coming of dawn, I decided to forego that pleasure. Instead, I sat down with my glass of milk in the comfort of my recliner, and reflected on what I'd been dreaming. Clearly, I could see that this dream had something to do with the stolen chart, the missing plane, the lost treasure, fishing, Jocko and his dog, and even maybe Ernie's death. I could see how all of these things had been incorporated into my dream. But, the one thing that I found surprising was that the riddle was somehow being hidden by a secret code. That solution was something that had never occurred to me before. Was the fact that it had occurred in this dream significant? Or, was it just as crazy as the possibility of being handed a book by an old grouper? That was the problem with trying to understand dreams- you never knew where things in them came from. But, now, for whatever reason, as soon as I'd finished my milk, my mind was comforted and I quickly dozed off in my chair.

Which is where I was still sleeping when the phone rang at seven that morning? Groggily I reached for it and drowsily answered- "hello."

"Good morning, Jim. I didn't wake you again, did I?"

I immediately recognized, hidden in Mike Collin's gruff voice, the tongue-in-cheek nature of his concern.

Not wanting to be out done I replied, "Of course not, Collins. In fact, we just got in after a night, along with all the other citizens of St. James City, of dancing nakedly in the streets, howling at the moon, and worshiping our village's pagan gods. It was a hell of a time. You should have been there!"

"Naked, huh? Sounds like fun, but probably better that I wasn't. Seriously, are you awake enough for some news?"

"Yeah, Mike. What you got?"

"Two things, Jim. First, Ernie was definitely murdered. It's a good thing you pushed us to look further. We found that he'd been slipped a "Mickey" just to cause him to sleep. Then we found that his heart attack had actually been caused by a drug injection."

"An injection! You mean somebody gave him a shot of something that killed him?"

"Exactly. Initially, the coroner couldn't find anything out of the ordinary. The normal blood work simply showed high levels of potassium, but apparently this is often normal with a heart attack. He explained that anytime a muscle in the body is severely damaged, and the heart is a muscle, unusually large amounts of potassium are released into the blood. It wasn't until the ME started to look for an injection mark that we stumbled onto what had actually happened."

"An injection mark? You mean like where a needle went in?"

"Yep. You want to guess where he found it?"

"Mike, I'd rather not. Why don't you just tell me?"

"Jeez, Jim, you sure are grumpy early in the morning- no fun at all."

"Collins, I'm sorry. But, I have had a rough night. Why don't you just tell me what you found?"

"The ME found the mark behind Ernie's left ear."

"A needle mark was behind his ear? Just one?"

"Yep. The ME found a single needle puncture there. But, clearly, a needle mark there was suspicious- and suggestive. It turns out that someone had administered an injection of potassium chloride to Ernie."

"Potassium chloride! Isn't that table salt?"

"Jim, you must not have done that good in high school chemistry? Table salt is sodium chloride, not potassium chloride. They are very similar compounds- both are crystalline, both dissolve easily, and both can be absorbed by humans and plants. But, that's about as far as the similarities go. Having said that, potassium chloride is fairly common. It's frequently found in medications, sometimes used as a salt substitute, and is even used as a water softener. Beyond this, however, it is often used as one of several drugs administered in lethal injections for executions. When injected in this form it causes the heart to stop beating, i.e., cardiac arrest. The ME told me that an injected overdose can cause severe heart arrhythmias, which quickly lead to heart spasms, which soon cause the heart to stop functioning altogether."

"Mike, is this stuff readily available? Or, is it hard to get?"

"It's not that hard to get hold of. It is frequently prescribed for patients who have a potassium deficiency. But, in this application it's usually in a dilute form just to help limit accidental overdoses. It's fairly difficult to acquire in a more highly concentrated form."

"So, was Ernie injected with a concentrated version?"

"Jim, we don't know. It could have been done either way. He could have been injected either with a concentrated form, or by a larger injection of a more dilute solution. Apparently, after injection there's really no sure way to tell which was administered."

"So, Mike, you're telling me that just about anyone could have gotten their hands on this?"

"No. It would have taken a little effort, and the right connections. But, it wouldn't have been all that hard to come up with a lethal dose."

"Great! Now, what's the other thing you wanted to tell me?"

"You still want to take a look at the chart that Ernie gave to your friend?"

"You're damn right I want to. Have you found it?"

"Yep. It's in my evidence locker right now in the sub-station. You can't take it, of course, but if you wanted to help me identify it as being the actual missing chart I might not notice you looking at it for a while."

"Unfortunately, Mike, I've never actually seen the chart. Would it be okay with you if Doc and I came together to ID the chart? Can we come this afternoon?"

"Sure. I've got no problem with that. Can ya'll come to the office in Pineland at three?"

"We'll make it happen. Now, how'd you find the chart?"

"I thought you'd be interested in that. After Ernie died I started to take what you'd told me about Jocko diving out in the Gulf more seriously. So, I got the judge to issue a warrant to search his boat. I found the chart in his chart locker."

"What about Jocko? Was he there when you searched?"

"No, he wasn't. His neighbors at the marina told me that he was out in the Gulf on a grouper boat. They'd been keeping his dog for him. After I found the chart we've been keeping an eye on his boat, and waiting for the grouper boat to come back in. But, unfortunately, when the boat docked last night Jocko was nowhere to be found. We're thinking that, after he saw our car in the parking lot, he probably dropped off the stern, and swam away. But, I'm not worried, we'll find him."

"So, Mike, do you think Jocko killed Ernie?"

"Jim, at this point, I don't see how. At least, not, if he was really out in the Gulf all week- and the crew on the boat says that he was. But, still, Jocko's acting strange, and we did find the chart on his boat. He's hiding something- for sure. We'll find out what that is when we get our hands on him."

"Mike, thanks for telling me this. I appreciate it."

"Jim, I appreciate your help, too. I'll see ya'll later."

Chapter Twenty Seven

I immediately called Doc. "Doc, there's been a slight change in plans. Mike Collins just called to tell me that he'd found your lost chart on Jocko's boat. He wants us to come up to the sub-station in Pineland this afternoon at three to identify it. Can you make it then?"

"Of course, I can. But, why'd Mike finally go to look on Jocko's boat?"

"He told me that after Ernie died he decided to take what we'd been telling him more seriously. And, it's a good thing he did. Mike said that the Medical Examiner had determined that Ernie, in fact, had been murdered. He said that he'd been drugged, and then injected behind the ear with potassium chloride. Apparently, this causes a fatal heart attack."

"Damn! So, does he think Jocko did it?"

"He's not sure. But, Jocko's is on the lam, and Mike is looking for him, as we speak."

"What do you mean he's on the lam?"

"Supposedly, he was out in the Gulf on a grouper boat all week. But, when the boat docked he wasn't on board. They are looking for him."

"So, Jim, what I'm hearing you say is that possibly Jocko could have murdered Ernie? And, now he's loose somewhere on the island?"

"Yeah- one more thing. Didn't Kenny say ya'll saw a grouper boat pass you yesterday while you were anchored over the treasure spot? I wonder if Jocko saw ya'll out there?"

"Jim, that boat was a mile away. He couldn't have known it was us."

"Doc, don't you have a set of binoculars on your boat?"

"Of course… Oh, I see what you mean!"

"Doc, I think we all need to keep our doors locked until they find Jocko. I'll pick you up at two forty."

I picked Doc up as arranged. As he got in he noticed the bag of nautical navigation tools that I'd brought with me.

"You need to plot a course to Pineland?," Doc asked.

"No. But, I've got a theory about the chart. I had a dream last night that involved a hidden code and that chart. Now, I don't have a clue about what it could be, but if it's on a chart it probably has something to do with a plotted position. So, that's why I brought this along. Mike will probably let us have about an hour to figure it out."

"That's not much time to break a code, Jim. How do you plan to go about it?"

"I don't have a clue. I guess we'll just have to take a look at the chart and see if anything jumps out."

Neither of us said anything else on the drive north to Pineland.

As we entered the door of the sub-station Mike Collins greeted us. He'd obviously been awaiting our arrival.

"Good afternoon, Gentlemen," he said. "Follow me. I've got the chart in the office."

Once we were inside, Mike closed the door, and said: "The chart's folded up on the desk. How long are ya'll going to want to look at it?"

"We're not sure, Mike. It might take us a while."

"I can give you an hour. No more than that. And, Jim what the hell is in that bag you brought in?"

"These are just my old navigation plotting instruments- a parallel ruler, a set of dividers, a nautical slide rule, some pencils, and a note pad."

"Jim, what are ya'll going to do with that stuff?"

"Don't know yet, Mike. Probably just take some readings and measurements off the chart. Will that be okay?"

"I don't see any problem with doing that. But, I think I'll stay in here with you just to make sure that's all you do. Now you better get started- the clock's ticking."

Doc and I cleared the inbox and phone off of the desk, and then spread the chart out on top of it. The chart was positioned with its top up, so that we were looking at the chart from south to north. The east, of course, was to the right, with the coast of Florida clearly defining the limits to navigation in that direction. To the west was the open Gulf. We could see a multitude of labeled locations indicated mid-way in the chart. Each was carefully marked with a small "x," which had been precisely circled, and then neatly labeled. I recognized some of the spots where we had fished. And, of course, my eyes were drawn to the spot labeled "B-26." But, other than that unusual nomenclature there was nothing that caused that location to appear different than any of the others that surrounded it. "Big Grouper; Carlos' Grouper Hole; Red Snapper #1; Grouper Rocks, etc." I was already becoming discouraged about being able to discover anything useful from this chart. I straightened up, stepped back, and let out a deep sigh.

"Doc, you see anything out of the ordinary? Anything that doesn't look quite right?"

"Nope. It just looks like an old fishing chart to me."

With that, Mike Collins interrupted. Ya'll mind if I take a look?"

"Go ahead. Anything look out of kilter to you?"

Mike stepped to the front of the desk, took in a deep breath, and gazed silently at the whole chart. It looked to me like he was just doing a broad overview of the chart, not really looking at any of the details or marks. After a moment, he stepped away and asked: "What about those two marks off to the east, close to the beach. The pattern of where they are located seems to be different from the others."

Doc and I bent back over to inspect those spots more closely. Truthfully, I remembered noticing them on Doc's GPS- but to me they'd always seemed too far inshore to hold much promise for serious grouper fishing so I'd never really focused on them. But, now I had to admit that Mike was right- these two spots didn't really fit with the pattern of all the others. Because of their very shallow locations they were definitely different. Then, as we looked more closely we could see that these spots were labeled in a slightly different way as well- for starters none of them referenced fish in anyway. There was no mention of grouper, snapper, or even any inshore species like sheepshead, or snook. These were simply labeled El Lobo 1; and El Lobo 2. But, other than these things we could see nothing about them that was unusual. They both marked shallow water locations. One was just a few hundred yards off shore. The other appeared to be maybe a mile off of the coast. There were no rocks formations nearby; no drop offs; in essence there was nothing that would indicate good fishing. There was only simple sandy bottom. These spots were definitely different. But, what they indicated was a mystery.

For the next twenty minutes we looked more closely at the chart. We looked at it from all angles; we even turned it over and looked at the back of the chart and studied where the book title had been printed. But, nothing jumped out at us- except for those unusual inshore locations. Eventually, we all began to become exasperated. Finally, Mike Collins decided that he'd had enough.

"Alright, Doc, I've about had enough of this fun. Is this your chart, or not?"

"Mike, it definitely is the chart that was given to me by Ernie. It is the chart that was stolen from my garage. Can I take it home now?"

"No, you can't. I've got to hold this as evidence against Jocko. But, eventually, after this all is finally resolved, you'll probably be able to get it back."

"Look, Mike," I interrupted. "There is something about this chart that we're supposed to figure out. There's something hidden on it that Ernie wanted us to know. I'm convinced that there's something on it that will probably help us to know who killed Ernie. We can't just stop now. We need to take it home until we can figure out what that is!"

"Jim, you can't do that. The chart has to stay in the possession of the Sheriff's Department. I'm taking it to the evidence unit this afternoon."

"Well, damn, Mike. I know there's something here. At least let me calculate the GPS coordinates of those two inshore spots before we have to go. That way I'll have something to work on."

"Get started. You've got ten minutes."

"Okay. Doc, hand me my instrument bag. I'll determine the coordinates, and you write them down."

I took out my parallel rules and divider, and then passed a note pad and pencil to Doc. The first spot I measured was "El Lobo 1," the northern most of the spots marked. I carefully used the divider to determine its distance from the nearest latitude line that was a little to the south of the spot. I then moved the divider to the legend on the eastern edge of the chart, and read the indicated latitude to Doc. Twenty six degrees, seventeen minutes, four seconds, north. Then I repeated the process, this time measuring the distance from the nearest longitude line. I carefully moved the divider to the top of the chart, taking care to measure as accurately as possible. When satisfied, I read off the measure of longitude: eighty one degrees, fifty minutes, twelve seconds, west.

After this I moved to "El Lobo 2." "Twenty six degrees, eight minutes, seven seconds, north. Eighty one degrees, fifty one minutes, ten seconds, west.

"Anything else you want to note before we leave?" Doc asked.

"I don't know if it's meaningful, but 'El Lobo 1' is right off Big Hickory Pass. 'El Lobo 2' is off Clam Pass."

Mike had patiently taken this in. But, he'd carefully been watching to make sure that we hadn't made any marks, erasures, or otherwise altered the chart. Finally, he spoke up. "Okay guys, ya'll have all you need? I've got to get going."

"We're good, Mike. Thanks for letting us do this," I said. "Don't know if it will lead to anything, but I appreciate you letting us do this."

"It seemed like the thing to do. Now, as I've said before- let me remind you guys that I don't want any of you interfering in this investigation- in any way. In fact, I've about had enough of being friendly and kind to the Pine Island branch of the Apple Dumpling Gang. If you find something, call me. Otherwise, please stay out my business. Caphiche?"

"Don't worry," Doc and I answered simultaneously.

On the drive south Doc and I discussed our next steps. But, neither of us had any ideas that sounded especially promising. Then, as I pulled into Doc's driveway, I mentioned that I really only had one idea that might have merit. He asked what it was.

"Well, I think that this somehow must have something to do with that book with its title written on the back of the chart. But, unfortunately, I don't know how. I've looked, and looked, at it, but haven't yet been able to see any connection. But, if something comes to me I'll let you know."

"Okay, Jim. Ya'll keep your doors locked."

Chapter Twenty Eight

Jill, when I came home was, of course, interested in what we'd learned. When I told her 'nothing' the look of disappointment on her face was obvious.

"Well, Jim, what are you going to do now?"

"Jill, if you don't have an objection, my plan is just to go downstairs, and think. Maybe something will come to me. Otherwise, I'm at a dead end."

"No objections on my part, Jim. Just don't wait too long to figure this out. I've about had enough of having to keep the doors locked. I prefer to just use the screen doors."

"Yeah, me too. Hopefully, I can come up with something. By the way, do you know anything about codes?"

"Unfortunately, not a thing, Babe."

"Thanks for the help." With that I exited the room, walking down the inside stairs. Once on the lower level I picked up my by now well-thumbed copy of 'A Dummies Guide to Home Repair.' I looked at its front cover; then at its back cover; and after that thumbed through the pages a few more times. But, just like all the others times that I'd done that- nothing jumped out at me. Next, I picked up my I-Pad, and, for lack of any better idea, typed in 'Book Code.' Wikipedia, of course, popped up as the first choice. I clicked on that, and read: *'A book code is a cipher in which the key is some aspect of a book or other piece of text.'* A paragraph later I read: *'Traditionally book ciphers work by replacing words in the plaintext of a message with the location of words from the book being used.'*

These words exploded in my brain. I felt like I'd just experienced an epiphany. Did this mean that the locations of the spots on the chart might indicate the position of words in the book? And, would those words tell us what it was that Ernie wanted us to know? Would it also help us understand why he had been killed? And, if we knew that, would we be able to figure out who had killed him?

I grabbed the book, and the paper on which Doc had copied down the GPS locations. The location of El Lobo 1 was 26 degrees, seventeen minutes, four seconds north/ 81 degrees, 50 minutes, 12 seconds west. So what could this mean? At first nothing came to me. I tried adding the numbers. I tried subtracting them. I was almost ready to start multiplying when an idea came to me. What if degrees simply corresponded to a page number? Could the minutes indicate a line on that page? And, did seconds show the specific word on that line? I opened the book to page 26, counted down 17 lines, and then found the 4th word- '*under.*' By itself that word didn't mean anything. But, at least I had been able to find a word using this method. For that I was excited

Now, what about the longitude measure? Would it produce a word as well? I opened the book to page 81, the 50th line, and found the 12th word- '*the.*' Again I had found a word, and, even better, a word that seemed to work grammatically with '*under.*' '*Under the* ....' I couldn't move to the coordinates of El Lobo 2 fast enough!

Again, I found page 26. This time I counted down 8 lines, and moved over to the 7th word- '*wood.*' '*Under the wood....*' Then I repeated the process with the longitude measure. I quickly thumbed open the book to page 81. Then counted down to the 51st line, and over to the 10th word. I could hardly breathe at what I then saw. Immediately, I knew that my hunch had been correct. The chart, and the book code, had led us to exactly the spot that Ernie had wanted us to find. That word was '*stack.*' Ernie wanted us to look for something '*under the wood stack.*'

Clearly, he must have hidden something there that he wanted us to find. Why else would he have given Doc the chart in the first place? Did this have something to do with the book that he said he'd written? Had Ernie had a chance, like he'd planned, to send that book to the editor of 'The News-Press'? From the way he'd been killed I didn't think that he'd had time to do that. But, had the murderer found the book? Clearly he'd ransacked the inside of the house looking for it. Had he known to look under the wood pile? Was the book still there?

After thinking about those questions, I started to call Mike Collins? But, for some reason that I didn't really understand, I didn't yet feel comfortable doing this. So, rather than calling Mike, I decided to call Doc and Kenny. I instructed them to meet me at Low Key Tiki in five minutes. With that I ran upstairs.

"Jill, I've got to go meet Doc and Kenny at Low Key Tiki."

"Why? Did you figure out something?"

"I thought about lying to her, but immediately I regretted having even considered the idea. Besides, I knew that she'd have instantly seen through that.

"Yeah. I think so. But, I want to run it by Doc and Kenny before I say anything. I'll be back soon."

"Jim- I don't like the sound of this."

"It'll be okay. But, Babe, you need to keep the doors locked a little longer. And, I'd appreciate it if you wouldn't go out anywhere by yourself."

"Oh, so you can go out by yourself, but I can't! Give me a break, Jim. We're in this together- remember?"

"Yeah. I'm sorry. I just want you to be careful? I'll be careful, too. I'll be back, soon."

Two minutes later I was sitting at a remote table on the canal-side deck at the Low Key Tiki- waiting for Doc and Kenny. I had deliberately chosen this spot- usually unpopular given it being out in the hot sun-since I knew that, even during after-work 'Happy Hour,' it would be difficult to be overheard from here. It would also be easy to see if anyone was paying us any undue attention.

Doc arrived in his truck shortly. Then, seconds later, Kenny, making his normal impossible to miss arrival, slid his golf car to a stop alongside Doc's truck. I waved. Together they walked to the table.

"Damn, Jim? Have you lost your mind sitting out here in the sun?" Kenny asked.

"Kenny, we need a little bit of privacy. I think I have figured out what Ernie's chart was all about? I think I now know why he wanted Doc to have it."

"Does this have anything to do with the lost treasure?" Kenny excitedly enquired.

"Truthfully, I don't know. But, I'm sure that this is about something Ernie wanted us to know- just in case something ever happened to him."

"Why us? Why did he give the chart to Doc?" Kenny asked.

"My guess," I said, "is that Ernie, like most, knew of our reputation on the island for solving mysteries. And, he knew that you, Doc and I hung out together. So, I suspect that he chose us to help him take care of things in case his primary plan fell apart."

At this point, Doc asked, "Jim, you said you'd found out something about the chart. What did you find?"

"I think I have broken Ernie's code. It was something that he knew that we'd eventually be able to solve since it was so simple, and since it had to do with fishing."

"Wait a minute, Jim!" Kenny exclaimed. "I'm not sure I like the way you said that. He thought we'd be able to break his code because it was 'so simple'?"

"No offense, Kenny. But, think about it. If it had been too hard we'd have just gone fishing, instead!"

"That's true," Kenny agreed.

"Okay, guys, let's get back to the matter at hand," Doc said. "Jim, educate us about how you've broken the code."

"I believe that those two spots that we got the coordinates for from the chart today actually represented a code. Clearly, they did not indicate good fishing spots- that much was obvious. What I now believe is that they were a code that told us where Ernie had hidden a book that he'd written- a book that was very important to Ernie. So important, in fact, that he wanted to have a backup plan in place for getting it to the press in case something happened to him."

"Jim, what the hell are you talking about?" Kenny asked. "What spots? What coordinates?"

I took a breath, realizing that we'd not yet told Kenny about the meeting we'd had today with Mike Collins, and about the numbers we'd taken from the chart. I brought him up to speed, and then explained to both about the book code, and what I'd uncovered using it.

"My question to both of you is what should we do about this? Should we call Mike Collins? Or, should look into it ourselves? Or, should we just do nothing?"

"Jim," Doc asked, "why shouldn't we just call Mike?"

"Well, he did tell us today to not get involved in his business," I said.

"But," Doc replied, "didn't we also promise today to tell him about anything we uncovered?"

"Not exactly," I replied. "We may have implied that, but my recollection is that we simply told him not to worry."

"Okay. But, really, why shouldn't we involve him?"

"I'm not sure, but I've just got a feeling that this is about something that Ernie didn't trust the cops to be involved with. He could have told the cops at any time. But, instead, he wanted to send this to the editor of 'The News-Press.' Who knows, Ernie may have done something that wasn't legal? He told me that he didn't want to put himself in jeopardy- legal or otherwise. And, who knows, maybe he did, and that was why he was killed."

"Okay, Jim," Kenny asked, "if we don't call Mike what *do* we do?"

"I just want to go find out what's under Ernie's wood pile. After that we'll make a decision about whether to call Mike Collins, or not. Ya'll want to help me?"

"Yeah,' they excitedly replied in unison.

"When do you want to go?" Doc asked.

"Tonight," I replied.

Doc said, "I can do that. How about you, Kenny? Are you in?"

"I can be, but I told Sweet William that I was going to try to get a card group together tonight."

"Kenny, what if we played it this way? Why don't you tell Janice that Doc and I are going with you to play cards? See if she will ask Peggy and Jill to come over and have dinner with her. Then, you can just put Sweet William off. You, Doc and I will go exploring instead."

"That should work," Kenny agreed. "But, how are we going to do this. Are all three of us just going to walk up on the wood pile and tear it down?"

"How about this plan?" I asked. Doc and I will ride up with you in your car. You can drop us off by the Calusa Museum- it's only a couple of blocks through the woods from there to Ernie's. That way Doc and I can sneak up in the dark, and take a look. In the meantime, you can ride around and keep a look out. If you see anything unusual you lay on your horn, and we'll take off. You can pick us up later in the parking lot outside of the museum. Does that make sense?"

"That should work," Doc replied. Where do we meet to get started?"

"I'll just pick you up at seven, just like I would if we were going to play cards," Kenny answered.

"What should we wear?" Doc asked.

"Wear something dark, and some gloves. We ought to at least try to look like spooks, or crooks, or something sinister."

"Sounds good," Doc said.

"And, it sounds like fun," Kenny answered.

"Let's hope," I replied. "But, let's not forget that somebody killed Ernie, and, likely killed him because of what we're going to be looking for tonight. I think we're getting into something serious."

"I'll bring my gun," Kenny replied.

Chapter Twenty Nine

A little before eight, Kenny pulled into the parking lot of the Randell Research Center. This University of Florida sponsored museum and exhibit is located where once one of the Calusa Indian's largest settlements was. Ponce de Leon and the other Spanish explorers were reportedly entertained on this very spot as the gold-hungry Conquistadors began their long, ultimately ill-fated, courtship of the Calusa. I felt a shiver run down my back as I thought about that history. I was hoping that any native ghosts that undoubtedly still resided here would elect to be on our sides tonight. Then, I quickly gave up that thought, understanding that it wasn't especially likely that they'd choose to align with a couple of descendents of the hated British, a group who had sponsored the invading Creek Indians to butcher, or enslave, the few weakened Calusa who survived their earlier encounters with the Spanish. Hopefully, these spirits would simply choose to remain neutral in tonight's adventure.

In the bright moonlight Doc and I were able to easily follow the marked trail that led through the Center's grounds in the general direction of Ernie's house. Once we reached the limit of that property we stepped onto well tended, neatly mowed grass that lay under the towering canopies of hundreds of nearly century-old Mango trees that comprised a large, deserted, orchard. A few hundred yards later we took a break, hiding in the middle of a thick stand of Brazilian Pepper bushes- a despised, rapidly growing invasive species that now flourishes throughout Pine Island. From this location we had a clear view of the back of Ernie's property. Twenty yards ahead of us was the outdoor concrete grill where he'd cooked us those delicious Cuban lunches. A few feet to the side of that was the stack of wood from which Ernie had fed the grill's fire. The stack looked exactly as we remembered it looking- the same height, the same length. From what we could tell it had not been disturbed. Doc and I silently nodded at each other as we finished our quick assessment.

He began to step out of the bushes when I laid my hand on his arm, and put my finger to my lips. I'd heard something- the sound of a car moving. We waited. Then, as we watched, we could see Kenny's Expedition slowly drive by the front of the house. Assured that he was doing his job, we moved on to ours.

I took the left side of the stack. Doc took the right. We'd brought along two medium Phillips head screwdrivers to use as probes, and using these we began to carefully work the ground beneath the neatly split oak. Our plan was to not disturb the stack unless we had to. We had progressed about a third of the way from each end when my screwdriver's tip struck something that was unmistakably metal. The very slight sound of metal on metal alerted Doc. He stopped what he had been doing, and focused instead on what I'd found. Quickly, I probed the area where I'd made contact, attempting to define the dimensions of what my screwdriver had impacted. I was quickly pleased to see that the probe indicated that there was likely a box underneath the stack- a box maybe a foot long, and four inches in depth. Given the wood on top I couldn't tell how wide the box was, but I guessed that it was big enough to contain a book. I nodded at Doc. He moved closer, and we began to silently dig alongside where I'd discovered the box. We didn't think that we'd have to disturb the stack of wood. A minute later I gently pulled a metal box from beneath the cords of oak. We quickly filled the hole in, spreading grass and leaves on top of where we'd just dug, hoping to disguise what we'd been doing.

I picked up the box, and we started to retrace our steps. But, after a few steps an unexpected noise startled us. There is something about the sound made by the hammer of a firearm being cocked that will focus one's attention. In this case, our interest was concentrated on running as quickly as possible. We took off in the direction of the thicket of Brazilian Peppers.

But, then, just as we'd taken our first steps, we heard the intrusive blaring of the horn on Kenny's Expedition. Obviously, he'd seen, or heard, something that had gotten his attention, too. Then, after we'd reached the shelter of the bushes, we could see that Kenny had turned on the lights of his truck, and had positioned it to point in the direction of a nearby car port, a structure located near where we thought the frightening sound had originated. Then, as we listened intently, we could hear the sound of footsteps running away from us. A plan that appealed to us, too. Doc and I took off in the opposite direction, zigzagging through the mango orchard.

As we ran we glanced back to see that Kenny had begun making a sweep with his truck of the streets around Ernie's house. But, we didn't hear anything that indicated he'd made contact. Minutes later we stepped out of the shadows of the Randell Center's parking lot as Kenny's truck pulled to a stop on the narrow road. Seconds later we were inside, with Kenny driving as rapidly as he dared along the narrow, winding, pot-holed road that ran alongside the Sound.

"Kenny," I gushed, "thank God you blew your horn when you did! Somebody was going to shoot us if you hadn't."

"I know," Kenny replied. "All I could see was the shadow in the moonlight of a hand holding what looked like a pistol. Seeing that scared the stew out of me. So, I decided to blow the horn. I was hoping that if I did that then whoever had the gun might not shoot you. I guess it worked."

"I guess," Doc agreed. "Where you able to see who it was?"

"No. I never saw anything other than that shadow. I heard his footsteps though. He was running fast. From what I could tell he was heading in the general direction of the marina. I tried to find him, but I never saw him. Did ya'll get what you were looking for?"

"Kenny," I answered, "I think so. We've got a metal box, but we haven't opened it yet. But, I'm willing to bet that it's what we were looking for. Probably what the shooter was looking for, too. Let's get home."

Chapter Twenty Nine

As we drove south on Stringfellow Road I called Jill and told her that we were heading in. I learned that the girls had gathered for dinner at Doc and Peggy's house. I told her that we'd meet them there.

As Kenny, Doc, and I walked into the house I don't know what kind of reaction I expected. But, it probably wasn't the guffaws of laughter that greeted us as they took in our carefully selected sleuthing wardrobes- apparently the carefully applied streaks of black make up on our faces, and our matching black t-shirts and jeans hadn't actually created the fearful sinister images that we'd been hoping for. But, these impressions rapidly transitioned to concern as they registered what these outfits implied we'd been doing.

"Oh, Jim, damn it, you told me that you'd be careful. What have ya'll been doing? And, are you okay?"

"Yeah, we're fine…."

My reply was interrupted by Peg asking, "What's in the box you're carrying?"

Doc looked at me, and Kenny, before replying, "Please, everyone just sit down, and we'll tell you where we've been."

Together we took the next five minutes to explain what we'd been up to.

"Okay," Peggy interrupted. "I've got it. But, again, what's in the box?"

"We don't know. But, let's find out," I answered.

I placed the container over the kitchen sink to brush off any residual dirt, and then sat it on a dish towel I'd spread on the counter. I was delighted, as I clicked the catch on the front of the box, to see that it wasn't locked. I gently lifted the lid, and looked inside. I saw a wrapped package. It was the right size for a book but it was bound in multiple layers of plastic wrap- apparently intended to protect what was inside from moisture. Impatiently, I began to un-wrap it. After unwinding a half-dozen turns of cling wrap I could make out what looked to be a simple, hand-lettered, cover of a book. The book itself looked to be almost two inches thick. Clearly, this was not a short story. But, when I tried to read the title I couldn't decipher what it said- it was written in Spanish: *'Matamos a Kennedy!'*.

I held it up, and asked, "Okay, Peg, you're the Spanish teacher- what does this title say?"

I could see her eyes widen, and then her right hand slowly moved up- and covered her mouth- as if it was trying to prevent hers from translating what she'd just seen. She then looked into my eyes- the look of concern even more obvious now.

"Peg?" I gently asked again.

She turned her head away, and looked at Doc. They stared intently at each other for a long moment. I knew that she wouldn't have needed to ask permission, or for approval- it was more as if they were simply willing a quiet strength to each other- strength for facing something that I didn't yet understand. I waited patiently.

She turned back in my direction and said nervously, "The title of the book is *We Killed Kennedy.*"

The silence of the room was instantly shattered. "What? Who killed Kennedy? Which Kennedy- John or Bobbie? Is this for real? Who wrote this book? What about Lee Harvey Oswald? Oh, my God!" These were just a few of the nearly simultaneous expressions that I could decipher from the ensuing tumult.

I held up my hands, and waited for the noise to subside. Finally, after several minutes, everyone eventually focused on me. Once I had their attention I said, "Ernie Valdez wrote this book. He told me just a few days ago that he'd written about something that he'd done- something about which he was extremely proud of having accomplished. Ernie said that he wanted, shortly before he expected to die, to mail this book to the Editor of the News Press. He also told me that there was only one copy of the book. He said that, if for some reason he couldn't get it to the newspaper, he didn't trust law enforcement to deal with it appropriately. It seems to me that Doc and I, apparently, were his backup plan in case something happened to him. So now, I guess, it's up to us to ensure that this book gets safely into the hands of the Editor."

"So, how are we going to do that?" Jill asked.

"Tomorrow, when the paper's office is open, I would suggest that we all drive into Ft. Myers, and hand it directly to the Editor- no one else. Then we can wash our hands of this affair, and feel good about having done what Ernie wanted us to do."

"Okay. But, can we read it first?" Kenny asked.

We all looked around at each other. From what I could see no one seemed opposed to the idea.

Then Peg said, "I can translate, and read it out loud".

I handed the book to her. She cleared a spot on the coffee table in front of the L-shaped sofa, and sat down. The rest of us settled into the couch's cushions, and waited expectantly for her to read.

She carefully opened the handwritten cover of the book, turned a page, and began to read the Dedication. *"This book, and all of the actions contained within, is dedicated to the memory of a great Cuban patriot, and my best friend- Juan Diaz. May he, and my other Cuban brothers who died on Playa Giron, rest in eternal peace. Your deaths have been avenged."*

"Who was Juan Diaz?" Janice asked.

"Beats me!" I replied. "Peg, what does Playa Giron mean?"

217

"Specifically, it's just Giron Beach," she replied. "But, I think that is the beach where part of the 'Bay of Pigs' invasion took place."

"That would make sense," I replied. "Keep reading."

Peg turned the page, and resumed: *"Preface: My name is Ernie Valdez. I am a Cuban, exiled in the United States of America since 1959. While I am now an American Citizen my love for the land of my birth remains as strong as ever. I have written this book to describe my role, and the roles of many others, in the planning for, and the successful assassination of, John Fitzgerald Kennedy, on November 22, 1963. This action, murderous as it may now seem, was taken in retribution for the preventable slaughters of so many of my Cuban brothers during the failure of our sacred mission to liberate Cuba at the Bay of Pigs, April 17, 1961. On that day we realized that we had all been betrayed by President Kennedy. For that duplicity I swore an oath over the dead body of my friend Juan Diaz that I would not let this act go unpunished. I didn't.*

At that time there were only three groups who wanted to see Kennedy dead. My exiled brothers and I, obviously, wished to respond to this treachery. But, we were not alone. The Central Intelligence Agency, and the American Mafia, each also had their own reasons for wishing Kennedy dead. They, too, both felt that they had also been betrayed.

The CIA understood that the President had intentionally caused the failure of the invasion, and further had deliberately sacrificed the lives of the invasion forces. Beyond that the Kennedys were clearly intent on destroying the Agency. The longtime, highly respected leader of the Agency had been removed, and made the scapegoat for the failure of the invasion. He had been replaced as Director with a Kennedy loyalist. It was understood that this was a mere prelude to the disbanding of the Agency.

The Mafia, for its part, had not only lost its extensive holdings and investments in Cuba, but it, too, felt that it had been misled by the Kennedys with respect to their support for recovering those assets. And, as if that wasn't bad enough, the new administration had aggressively begun to target the Mob, and its leaders, for prosecution. This anger reached a crescendo when Attorney General Bobby Kennedy had Carlos Marcello, the powerful and influential head of the New Orleans crime family, seized and extradited to Guatemala on what were obviously trumped up charges. These accusations were quickly overturned, and Marcello returned to New Orleans. Unsurprisingly, it wasn't long before he, Santo Trafficante (the head of Florida's mob), and Jimmy Hoffa (the targeted head of the Teamsters Union- the Mob's useful money laundering arm) began planning how best to eliminate the Kennedys.

All of these groups wanted Kennedy killed. But, initially, none felt that they could proceed alone. The risks were, simply, too high. But, those risks began to be reduced once Kennedy's opposition to the Viet Nam war became apparent. Concerns on the part of the traditionalists within the government grew with the delivery of his infamous "Peace Speech" in June of 1963. And, then, once Kennedy became entangled in an extra-marital affair with Mary Pinchot Meyer, and it became known that together they were doing drugs in the White House (including marijuana and LSD) the 'deep-state's' restraints on the CIA, the Mob, and Cuban Exile Community effectively dissolved. The order was passed through appropriate channels to implement the assassination plan.

At that time I, like many of my brothers in the Cuban exile community, clandestinely worked for the CIA. We had worked tirelessly to undermine and weaken the Castro regime. Now, I, and a few others, were selected to assist with what we later learned was the planned assassination of the President.

This is my account of that effort. I have included names, dates, and events that will assist honest researchers to document this story. Since that fateful day in 1963, what really happened has been covered up by the US government. But, now, as I near my own death, I am no longer willing to participate in that deception. While I swore an oath to the CIA, upon the penalty of death, to never divulge this story, I feel that the oath I made to my dead friend Juan Diaz trumps that obligation. I want to honor my friend's memory by letting the world to know what happened, and why. And, more than anything else, I want freedom for Cuba. I hope this story- the truth- will help to bring that about. Cuba Libre!

Peg looked up, signaling that she had reached the end of the Preface. For several moments no one spoke- it was obvious that

219

each was trying to process the implications of what they'd just heard. Jill responded first.

"My, God! This is important. This could completely rewrite history!"

Then, just as these words had come out of her mouth, a black clad, masked gunman stepped into the room through the open sliding door from the screened lanai.

"I don't think history will need to be rewritten" he said. "Please hand me that book."

After I recovered from the shock of the intruder's unexpected entry I noticed the weapon that he was menacingly pointing in our direction. While I'm no expert on firearms I could tell that it was a semi-automatic pistol. I thought the fact that it was equipped with a silencer, and a laser sight, was more than a little concerning. From the gun's cold blue-steel, recently-oiled sheen I gathered that it had been well maintained, and deduced that consequently it would be effective, and deadly. I guessed it was an expensive, government-issued weapon- probably a Sig Sauer. I noticed an expanded magazine that protruded slightly beneath the butt of the gun- undoubtedly an accessory that held enough rounds to take care of all of us. From the nature of the weapon it was obvious to me that our intruder wasn't a run of the mill burglar, and wouldn't be an easy man to overcome. We were in trouble.

Then I looked up from the gun and took more comprehensive look. He was a slim, well conditioned guy. There wasn't an ounce of fat. And, while I couldn't see his face, due to the sheer stocking-like material that stretched over his face and covered all but his eyes, I deduced from a slight stoop in his shoulders that he wasn't a young man- he could have even been elderly. But, the weapon in his steady hand made that qualification largely irrelevant. His clothing was uniformly black and (unlike the haphazardly thrown together TV-spook outfits that Doc, Kenny and I were wearing) looked to have been well tailored, comfortably fitted, and expensively manufactured. Likely a professional's uniform that had been used before. The only part of this attire that seemed the least different from what one might expect an accomplished assassin to be wearing were his pair of worn, but well-shined, boat shoes. But, then again, maybe in Pine Island that's what hit men wear. Just as I was contemplating this I heard Kenny's angry voice.

"Jocko, God Damn your sorry ass. What the hell do you want now? We don't have your stupid chart! And, we haven't stolen your pirate treasure. Why don't you just get the hell out of here?"

The gun man swung the muzzle of his weapon towards Kenny. Its laser was now centered on Kenny's forehead. Knowing the volatile nature of Kenny's temper I didn't like what was going down. I decided to interrupt.

"Kenny, our friend here isn't Jocko. This guy, as you can see, is in very good shape. And, Jocko, even though he's about the same height, easily weighs sixty or seventy pounds more. This fellow is certainly not Jocko. But, unless I'm badly mistaken, I think I do know who this is. Kenny, allow me to introduce you to Mr. Robert Barnes, current resident of Useppa Island, and, I believe, a retired decorated agent of the CIA."

Now I noticed that the laser dot had swung from Kenny's head to mine. But, at least I'd succeeded in getting the gunman's attention from Kenny. Having achieved at least that small success I decided that my best option, in fact my only course of action, was to keep talking and hope that something positive might develop.

"Mr. Barnes, we haven't actually been introduced, but my name is Jim Story. The lady to my right is my wife Jill. You've already met Kenny. His wife, Janice, is sitting on the far end of the sofa. The fellow sitting next to her is Doc. His wife Peg, sitting on the table, has been reading a most interesting story to us. This, by the way, is their beautiful house. It's very nice, isn't it? Now, I'm sure that Doc and Peg regret not having delivered an invitation to you to join us tonight, but they simply didn't know that you were interested. But still, I'm sure that they didn't mean to be impolite. And, now, since you're here, can they offer you a drink? Scotch? Rum? Wine? Beer? Peg mixes some excellent Chocolate Old Fashions? What'll it be?"

"Mr. Story, how'd you recognize me?"

"I was with Ernie on Useppa a few days ago. I saw you two talking. And, I noticed your shoes- you do know, don't you, that not everyone in these parts spit shines their boat shoes!"

"Mr. Story- proper men take care of their footwear. But, you're right- down here not many routinely polish their shoes. And, that oversight drives me nuts. But, I have to say that it was observant on your part to have noticed my shoes. I appreciate that you did."

Having successfully established some degree of relationship with the gunman, I decided that I might as well swing for the fence. "Robert (may I call you that?), I understand that Gentlemen wish the efforts that they make to groom and present themselves properly will, at least, be recognized and appreciated. I'm glad that I was able, in some small way, to please you by noticing the difference it makes to your appearance. Now, before we go any further I was wondering if I could ask you one small question?"

Barnes didn't reply. But, his disguised head nodded slightly.

"Thank you," I replied. "Robert, I didn't mean to pry, but I noticed that you and Ernie argued when you were together on Useppa. Was what you argued about so important that you had to kill him?"

"Yes. It was. Ernie had sworn an oath to the CIA to never divulge any information about the Agency's involvement in the Kennedy assassination. I knew that he had sworn that oath because I was the agent who had administered it. I expected him to keep it. When I learned from a mutual friend that he had written a book that would disclose the story of our involvement I knew that I had to confront him about it, and remind him about his oath. That day, despite that reminder, he told me that it was his intention to disclose to the press what had happened, and why.

He explained that he couldn't go to his grave knowing that what had really happened was still being covered up. He felt that maintaining his silence, after all these years, was a betrayal to the honor of those who had given their lives at The Bay of Pigs. When I reminded him about the penalty for breaking his oath he simply smiled. It was clear then that he no longer feared death. When we were through arguing he told me that he was going to do what he had to do; I told him that I was going to do what I had to do. At that, we shook hands, embraced, and said good bye."

"What about when you came to his house?" I asked.

Barnes smiled. "I simply asked him for the book. He calmly told me that I'd never find it. After that we drank rum together- we even poured each other rounds. I don't know if he knew what I was doing, or not. But, clearly, he didn't drug me- even though he could easily have done so. I guess he was done fighting."

"So, you killed him then?"

"I was my obligation," Barnes answered stiffly.

As he said this Peg spoke. "Mr. Barnes would you like one of my Old Fashions now?"

I noticed that the laser dot had now moved to her forehead. "Thank you very much for the hospitality. But, no, I'm afraid, now is not a good time for a drink. Please just hand me the book."

Peg did as she was asked. With the book on the table in front of him, Barnes pulled the stocking mask from of his face. "I know, of course, that I shouldn't let you actually see my face. But, since Mr. Story has already disclosed my identity, it doesn't really matter that you could, at least theoretically, be able to identify me. Now, if you don't mind, I would appreciate it very much if you would all please turn around, move to the wall, and stand with your faces to it."

Everyone stood up. Most seemed unsure about what they should do next. Kenny, however, didn't hesitate. He instantly reached for the revolver that was hidden in the hip holster under the waistband of his exercise pants. He had only begun to get the weapon partially clear from its holster when Barnes fired. I could see that Kenny had been hit in the head. The impact of the round knocked him violently backwards, flipping him over the upholstered chair on which he'd previously been sitting. There was no doubt in my mind that Kenny had been killed by a shot to the head. I turned back towards Barnes. Now, there was no way that I was going to give him the opportunity to shoot any of us in the back. I had just begun to lean towards him, in preparation for making a lunge, when I heard the next shot.

Chapter Thirty

But, somehow this noise was less loud than the round that had previously been fired at Kenny. And, in the instant that it took me to process this difference my brain was also having trouble comprehending what it was actually seeing. I suppose that I had been expecting to witness Barnes firing calmly, deliberately, working down the line killing me, my wife, and my friends. What I had not been expecting was to see the side of Barnes' temple erupt in a geyser of red fluid.

It was certain that someone had shot him. But, who had done it? Barnes' weapon was still in his hand, it was lazily pointed generally in our directions, even while he collapsed lifelessly into a limp pile. I instinctively looked back to where Kenny had fallen-half expecting him to have taken the shot that had rescued us. But, as I looked it was clear that he hadn't fired the shot that had killed Barnes, either. My heart broke when I saw that Kenny was still lying exactly where he had fallen earlier, blood now pooling beneath his head. To me he looked dead.

I then swiveled around to look at the others. Jill and Janice were on the floor. Peg was still sitting on the coffee table- hands covering her mouth. Doc was standing. He looked to be in as much of a state of confusion as I. He looked at me and simply shrugged his shoulders, as if to say that he didn't know what had happened either.

I had just begun to step towards Barnes' body, planning to pick up his weapon so that at least we'd have some protection when three black clothed, heavily armed men silently stepped through the open sliding doors of the lanai. One of them motioned, with what looked like a tactical sniper's weapon, for me to move away from Barnes' body and weapon. He then picked up the book and, as he held his weapon on me, handed it to one of the other members of the team who put it in his backpack. They repeated the same process with Barnes' weapon. Then, without having said a word, the other two team members seized Barnes' body, a strong hand grabbing each lifeless arm. They drug the body quickly out the lanai, through the screen door, and towards the canal. I then heard what sounded like they dropped the body into some type of boat. From the muffled thump it made as it landed I guessed that the boat was probably an inflatable.

The black clad figure who remained in the room then said: "You will be safe now, and an ambulance has been called for your friend. But, you need to stay here until it arrives. Don't call anyone, and do not try to follow us. As long as you do what I've instructed you will be safe, and your friend will be cared for. Once the ambulance arrives, you may call the authorities. We should be gone by then. Good night."

"But," I blurted, "what about the book? What's going to happen to it?"

"What book?" he replied. Then he, too, was gone.

I couldn't even hear the sound of the engine on the inflatable as it rapidly disappeared.

Once the mystery man was gone I looked in Kenny's direction. Jill and Doc were kneeling beside him. Jill was wiping blood from his face, while Doc was feeling for a pulse. Peg was holding Janice, trying to comfort her.

"How is he?" I asked Doc.

"He's hurt, but I think he's breathing!" Doc replied.

"You *think* he's breathing?" I asked. "You can't tell?"

"No. But, I've got a pulse- a very weak pulse."

Moments later we heard the siren sound of the ambulance approaching the northern limits of St. James City. A minute longer and the ambulance with its strobe-like flashing red lights was parked in front of the house, and two medics were taking charge of Kenny. As we moved out of their way we could hear the sound of helicopters in the vicinity.

One of the medics then spoke, "he's alive, but critical. That's the MediVac chopper that we ordered. We're going to take him to York Road to meet it."

I could hear a helicopter landing to the north. But, I also thought I could hear what could have been another chopper off to the south, well out in the Bay. I assumed that meant that I could now safely call Lt. Collins. I scrolled through the contact list on my phone, and touched his number. It had only rung twice, without an answer, when Collins walked in the front door of the house.

"Hang up the phone, Story. I'm already here. Who's that on the floor?"

"It's Kenny. He's been shot."

"How's he doing?" Collins asked.

"Head wound, but at least the medics say he's alive."

"That's good. Everyone else okay?"

"Yeah- we're all fine," I replied.

"Now, here's what's going to happen," Collins said. "All of you are going to ride with my deputies to the hospital. They'll stay with you until you know what's going to happen with Kenny. They'll bring you home once you're ready to come."

"You don't have to do that, Mike," I said. "We can drive ourselves."

"I know that Jim, but, like I said, that's not what's going to happen. You all are going to ride with my deputies, and you are going to stay at the hospital until they bring you home. We've got some work to do here. Do you understand?"

"Not really," I replied. "But, it sounds to me like we are being kidnapped by the County."

"Lee County doesn't kidnap. But, we do detain folks to keep them from being in the way of the work that we've got to do. So, ya'll just go get in the cars with the Deputies while the medics load Kenny in the ambulance. I want you out of here as soon as he is. Janice will ride with Kenny in the chopper. The rest of you will meet them at Lee Memorial. Don't call me- I'll call you."

"But, what about the body?" I asked. "Don't you care that somebody got shot?"

"What body?" Collins replied coldly, turning away as he spoke. He then told the Deputies to get us all loaded in the patrol cars. It was clear than that my conversation with Collins was over. As we climbed into the cars I could see a number of sterile clothed technicians exit from Sherriff's Department vans and begin entering the house. They were carrying what looked like a vacuum cleaner, a bucket, and disinfecting equipment.

Chapter Thirty One

Three hours later, we were all gathered around Kenny as he lay quietly in his hospital bed. By this time Kenny's head had been cleaned and bandaged. There was now a breathing tube inserted up his nose, an intravenous drip was attached to a needle stuck into his arm, and assorted monitors where connected to quietly blinking electronic displays. Kenny was now dressed in a blue, open-backed, hospital gown. His head and upper body where slightly elevated in an uncomfortable-looking, adjustable bed. But, he was sleeping soundly, obviously under the influence of some type of effective sedative.

Doc, Peg, Janice, Jill and I were sitting, or standing, around Kenny as he slumbered. Our attendant deputies were patiently awaiting their orders outside in the hall. For our part, we were anticipating the arrival of the surgeon who had attended Kenny in the ER. The nurses who had taken care of him since he'd arrived in the room had not been forthcoming with any information. But, they had promised that the doctor's arrival was imminent. A half hour later the doctor came in. He was a spitting image of a tired-looking, slightly younger version of TV's Patrick Dempsey. From the haggard look on his face he'd probably had a busy evening. For our part, we appreciated him taking the time to update us.

After introductions, he quickly down got to business, saying: "This is a very lucky man. The bullet only glanced off of his skull, and dug a trench in his scalp. But, fortunately, there was no entry into the cranial cavity. He did lose a good amount of blood but, otherwise, he is uninjured. He'll likely have a severe headache when he wakes up, and we'll want to monitor him for a couple of days to ensure that there are not any cognitive issues. He'll have some healing to do and will always have a scar. But, I think in a few days he'll be home and, essentially, he'll be back to normal."

"Doctor!" Janice exclaimed, "that is such great news. Thank you so very much."

"It's is my pleasure, Ma'am. It's not often that I get to deliver good news. I'm glad that I can in this case. If you don't mind me asking, how did he come to being shot? From what I can see in this room it doesn't appear that a domestic dispute was the probable cause."

"Doctor," I spoke up, "this was definitely not a domestic dispute. I guess you could say that what occurred was an armed home invasion. My friend here tried to shoot the man who entered the house. But, unfortunately, he got shot instead."

"Well, I'll say it again. Your friend is a very lucky man. A centimeter or two difference and we'd be having a much unhappier conversation. What about the man he shot?"

"He wasn't as lucky," I replied. The Sheriff is investigating now.

The doctor nodded. Then, as soon as he'd left, we each took turns giving Janice a hug. I guess that we were all so relieved at the news we'd just received that we hadn't noticed that Kenny had come to.

"Looks like you're having a party in here!" we heard him say. "How about one of you good looking ladies hugging on me for a while? After all, I'm the one who got shot."

"Kenny!" we all cried out at nearly the same time, quickly huddling around his bed. Janice gave him a big kiss, as the rest of us began patting him affectionately.

"Hey," he exclaimed, "Ya'll better calm down, or you're going to hurt my head. It feels bad enough already! And, I don't l want my blood pressure to get so elevated that those machines start beeping!"

With that we tried to be gentle. But, I've got to say that Janice was still kissing Kenny just as affectionately as before.

This went on for a few minutes longer before a nurse entered the room. She advised us that it was time for Kenny's medications, and that it would probably be a good idea for us to leave so that Kenny could get some rest.

With the deputies hovering outside and looking through the door, nodding their obvious agreement with the nurse's suggestion, we concurred, and each took turns wishing Kenny 'good night.' Since I was in a corner of the room, I was the last to leave. But, as I stepped towards the door, I saw Kenny wave me over. As I neared he motioned with his fingers for me to lean even closer.

As soon as I was near, he said, "Did I get the bastard, Jim? Did I kill him? Ya'll are all okay, so I guess I shot him- right?"

I didn't say anything for a couple of seconds, considering what was the right thing to say.

Then I whispered, "Yeah, you got him alright, Kenny. The bastard is dead."

"Good. I didn't want ya'll to get hurt."

I patted Kenny's arm. "Thanks Buddy. Now you get a good night's sleep. You need to rest up so that we can go fishing."

Made in the USA
Lexington, KY
19 March 2019